KOREAN FAIRY TALES

KOREAN FAIRY TALES

BY

WILLIAM ELLIOT GRIFFIS

Author of "Korea: Within and Without"; "Korea: The Hermit Nation"
and of Japanese, Dutch, Belgian, Swiss
and Welsh Fairy Tales

NEW YORK
THOMAS Y. CROWELL COMPANY
PUBLISHERS

CONTENTS

A NOTE TO THE FRIENDS OF KOREA

Everywhere on earth the fairy world of each country is older and perhaps more enduring than the one we see and feel and tread upon. So I tell in this book the folk lore of the Korean people, and of the behavior of the particular kind of fairies that inhabit the Land of Morning Splendor. Yet, if I live long enough, I shall write the wonderful history of the Korean nation and civilization, which once so enriched Asia, and made possible the modern Japan such as we know today, of which fact the literature and art of both countries bear ample witness.

W. E. G.

THE UNMANNERLY TIGER

"Mountain Uncle" was the name given by the villagers to a splendid striped tiger that lived among the highlands of Kang Wen, the long province which from its cliffs overlooks the Sea of Japan. Hunters rarely saw him, and among his fellow-tigers the Mountain Uncle boasted that, though often fired at, he had never been wounded; while as for traps- he knew all about them and laughed at the devices used by man to catch him and to strip him of his coveted skin. In summer he kept among the high hills and lived on fat deer. In winter, when heavy snow, biting winds, and terrible cold kept human beings within doors, old Mountain Uncle would sally forth to the villages. There he would prowl around the stables, the cattle enclosures, or the pig pens, in hopes of clawing and dragging out a young donkey, a fat calf, or a suckling pig. Too often he succeeded, so that he was the terror of the country for leagues around.

One day in autumn, Mountain Uncle was rambling among the lower hills. Though far from any village, he kept a sharp lookout for traps and hunters, but none seemed to be near. He was very hungry and hoped for game.

But on coming round a great rock, Mountain Uncle suddenly saw in his path some feet ahead, as he thought, a big tiger like himself.

He stopped, twitched his tail most ferociously as a challenge, showed fight by growling, and got ready to spring. What was his surprise to see the other tiger doing exactly the same things. Mountain Uncle was sure there would be a terrible struggle, but this was just what he wanted, for he expected to win.

But after a tremendous leap in the air he landed in a pit and all of a heap, bruised and disappointed. There was no tiger to be seen, but instead a heavy lid of logs had closed over his head with a crash and he lay in darkness. Old Mountain Uncle was caught at last. Yes, the hunter had concealed the pit with sticks and leaves, and on the upright timbers, covered with vines and brushwood, had hung a looking-glass. Mountain Uncle had often beheld his own face and body in the water, when he stooped to drink, but this time not seeing any water he was deceived into thinking a real tiger wanted to fight him.

By and by, a Buddhist priest came along, who believed in being kind to all living creatures. Hearing an animal moaning, he opened the trap and lifting the lid saw old Mountain Uncle at the bottom licking his bruised paw.

"Oh, please, Mr. Man, let me get out. I'm hurt badly," said the tiger.

Thereupon the priest lifted up one of the logs and slid it down, until it rested on the bottom of the pit. Then the tiger climbed up and out. Old Mountain Uncle expressed his thanks volubly, saying to the shaven head:

"I am deeply grateful to you, sir, for helping me out of my trouble. Nevertheless, as I am very hungry, I must eat you up."

The priest, very much surprised and indignant, protested against such vile ingratitude. To say the least, it was very bad manners and entirely against the law of the mountains, and he appealed to a big tree to decide between them.

The spirit in the tree spoke through the rustling leaves and declared that the man should go free and that the tiger was both ungrateful and unmannerly.

Old Mountain Uncle was not satisfied yet, especially as the priest was unusually fat and would make a very good dinner. However, he allowed the man to appeal once more and this time to a big rock.

"The man is certainly right venerable Mountain Uncle, and you are wholly wrong," said the spirit in the rock. "Your master, the Mountain Spirit, who rides on the green bull and the piebald horse to punish his enemies, will certainly chastise you if you devour this priest. You will be no fit messenger of the Mountain Lord if you are so ungrateful as to eat the man who saved you from starvation or death in the trap. It is shockingly bad manners even to think of such a thing."

The tiger felt ashamed, but his eyes still glared with hunger; so, to be sure of saving his own skin, the priest proposed to make the toad a judge. The tiger agreed.

But the toad, with his gold-rimmed eyes, looked very wise, and instead of answering quickly, as the tree and rock did, deliberated a long time. The priest's heart sank while the tiger moved his jaws as if anticipating his feast. He felt sure that Old Speckled Back would decide in his favor.

"I must go and see the trap before I can make up my mind," said the toad, who looked as solemn as a magistrate. So all three leaped, hopped, or walked to the trap. The tiger, moving fast, was there first, which was just what the toad, who was a friend of the priest, wanted. Besides, Old Speckled Back was diligently looking for a crack in the rocks near by.

So while the toad and the tiger were studying the matter, the priest ran off and saved himself within the monastery gates. When at last Old Speckled Back decided against Mountain Uncle and in favor of the man, he had no sooner finished his judgment than he hopped into the rock crevice, and, crawling far inside defied the tiger, calling him an unmannerly brute and an ungrateful beast, and daring him to do his worst.

Old Mountain Uncle was so mad with rage and hunger that his craftiness seemed turned into stupidity. He clawed at the rock to get at the toad, but Speckled Back, safe within, only laughed. Unable to do any harm, the tiger flew into a passion of rage. The hotter his temper grew, the more he lost his wit. Poking his nose inside the crack he rubbed it so hard on the rough rock that he soon bled to death.

When the hunter came along he marveled at what he saw, but he was glad to get rich by selling the tiger's fur, bones, and claws; for in Korea nothing sells so well as a tiger. As for the toad, he told to several generations of his descendants the story of how he outwitted the old Mountain Uncle.

TOKGABI AND HIS PRANKS

Tokgabi is the most mischievous sprite in all Korean fairy-land. He does not like the sunshine or outdoors, and no one ever saw him on the streets.

He lives in the sooty flues that run under the floors along the whole length of the house, from the kitchen at one end of it to the chimney hole in the ground at the other end. He delights in the smoke and smut, and does not mind fire or flame, for he likes to be where it is warm. He has no lungs, and his skin and eyes are both fire-proof. He is as black as night and loves nothing that has white in it. He is always afraid of a bit of silver, even if it be only a hairpin.

Tokgabi likes most to play at night in the little loft over the fireplace. To run along the rafters and knock down the dust and cobwebs is his delight. His favorite game is to make the iron rice-pot lid dance up and down, so that it tumbles inside the rice kettle and cannot easily be got out again. Oh, how many times the cook burns, scalds, or steams her fingers in attempting to fish out that pot lid when Tokgabi has pushed it in! How she does bless the sooty imp!

But Tokgabi is not always mischievous, and most of his capers hurt nobody. He is such a merry fellow that he keeps continually busy, whether people cry or laugh. He does not mean to give any one trouble, but he must have fun every minute, especially at night.

When the fire is out, how he does chase the mice up and down the flues under the floor, and up in the garret over the rafters! When the mousies lie dead on their backs, with their toes turned upward, the street boys take them outdoors and throw them up in the air. Before the mice fall to the ground, the hawks swoop down and eat them up. Many a bird of prey gets his breakfast in this way.

Although Tokgabi plays so many pranks, he is kind to the kitchen maids. When after a hard day's work one is so tired out that she falls asleep, he helps her to do her hard tasks.

Tokgabi washes their dishes and cleans their tables for good servants; so when they wake up the girls find their work done for them. Many a fairy tale is told about this jolly sprite's doings-how he gives good things to the really nice people and makes the bad ones mad by spitefully using them. They do say that the king of all the Tokgabis has a museum of curiosities and a storehouse full of gold and gems and fine clothes, and everything sweet to eat for good boys and girls and for old people that are kind to the birds and dumb animals. For bad folks he has all sorts of things that are ugly and troublesome. He punishes stingy people by making them poor and miserable.

The Tokgabi king has also a menagerie of animals. These he sends to do his errands rewarding the good and punishing naughty folks. Every year the little almanac with red and green covers tells in what quarter of the skies the Tokgabi king lives for that year, so that the farmers and country people will keep out of his way and not provoke him. In his menagerie the kind creatures that help human beings are the dragon, bear, tortoise, frog, dog and rabbit. These are all man's friends. The cruel and treacherous creatures in Tokgabi's menagerie are the tiger, wild boar, leopard, serpent, toad and cat. These are the messengers of the Tokgabi king to do his bidding, when he punishes naughty folks.

The common, every-day Tokgabi plays fewer tricks on the men and boys and enjoys himself more in bothering the girls and women. This, I suppose, is because they spend more time in the house than their fathers or brothers. In the Land of Rat-tat-tat, where the sound of beating the washed clothes never ceases, Tokgabi loves to get hold of the women's laundry sticks which are used for pounding and polishing the starched clothes. He hides them so that they cannot be found. Then Daddy makes a fuss because his long white coat has to go without its usual gloss, but it is all Tokgabi's fault.

Tokgabi does not like starch because it is white. He loves to dance on Daddy's big black hat case that hangs on the wall. Sometimes he wiggles the fetich, or household idol, that is suspended from the rafters. But, most of all, he enjoys dancing a jig among the dishes in the closet over the fireplace, making them rattle and often tumble down with a crash.

Tokgabi likes to bother men sometimes too. If Daddy should get his topknot caught in a rat hole, or his head should slip off his wooden pillow at night and he bump his nose, it is all Tokgabi's fault. When anything happens to a boy's long braid of hair, that hangs down his back and makes him look so much like a girl, Tokgabi is blamed for it. It is even said that naughty men make compacts with Tokgabi to do bad things, but the imp only helps the man for the fun of it. Tokgabi cares nothing about what mortal men call right or wrong. He is only after fun and is up to mischief all the time, so one must watch out for him.

The kitchen maids and the men think they know how to circumvent Tokgabi and spoil his tricks. Knowing that the imp does not like red, a young man when betrothed wears clothes of this bright color. Tokgabi is afraid of shining silver, too, so the men fasten their topknots together, and the girls keep their chignons in shape, with silver hairpins. The magistrates and government officers have little storks made of solid silver in their hats, or else these birds are embroidered with silver thread on their dresses. Every one who can afford them uses white metal dishes and dresses in snowy garments. Tokgabi likes nothing white and that is the reason why every Korean likes to put on clothes that are as dazzling as hoar frost. Tons and mountains of starch are consumed in blanching and stiffening coats and skirts, sleeves and stockings. On festival days the people look as if they were dipped in starch and their garments encrusted in rock candy. In this manner they protect themselves from the pranks of Tokgabi.

EAST LIGHT AND THE BRIDGE OF FISHES

Long, long ago, in the region beyond the Everlasting White Mountains of Northern Korea, there lived a king who was waited on by a handsome young woman servant. Every day she gladdened her eyes by looking southward, where the lofty mountain peak which holds the Dragon's Pool in its bosom lifts its white head to the sky. When tired out with daily toil she thought of the river that flows from the Dragon's Pool down out of the mountain. She hoped that some time she would have a son that would rule over the country which the river watered so richly.

One day while watching the mountain top she saw coming from the east a tiny bit of shining vapor. Floating like a white cloud in the blue sky it seemed no bigger than an egg. It came nearer and nearer until it seemed to go into the bosom of her dress. Very soon she became the mother of a boy. It was indeed a most beautiful child.

But the jealous king was angry. He did not like the little stranger. So he took the baby and threw it down among the pigs in the pen, thinking that this would be the last of the boy. But no! the sows breathed into the baby's nostrils and their warm breath made it live.

When the king's servants heard the little fellow crowing, they went out to see what made the noise, and there they beheld a happy baby not seeming to mind its odd cradle at all. They wanted to give him food at once but the angry king ordered the child to be thrown away, and this time into the stable. So the servants took the boy by the legs and laid him among the horses, expecting that the animals would tread on him and he would be thus put out of the way.

But no, the mares were gentle, and with their warm breath they not only kept the little fellow from getting cold, but they nourished him with their milk so that he grew fat and hearty.

When the king heard of this wonderful behavior of pigs and horses, he bowed his head toward Heaven. It seemed the will of the Great One in the Sky that the boy baby should live and

grow up to be a man. So he listened to its mother's prayers and allowed her to bring her child into the palace. There he grew up and was trained like one of the king's sons. As a sturdy youth, he practiced shooting with bow and arrows and became skilful in riding horses. He was always kind to animals. In the king's dominions any man who was cruel to a horse was punished. Whoever struck a mare so that the animal died, was himself put to death. The young man was always merciful to his beasts.

So the king named the youthful archer and horseman East Light, or Radiance of the Morning and made him Master of the Royal Stables. East Light, as the people liked to say his name, became very popular. They also called him Child of the Sun and Grandson of the Yellow River.

One day while out on the mountains hunting deer, bears, and tigers, the king called upon the young archer to show his prowess in shooting arrows. East Light drew his bow and showed skill such as no one else could equal. He sent shaft after shaft whistling into the target and brought down both running deer and flying birds. Then all applauded the handsome youth. But instead of the king's commending East Light, the king became very jealous of him, fearing that he might want to seize the throne. Nothing that the young man could do seemed now to please his royal master.

Fearing he might lose his life if he remained near the king, East Light with three trusty followers fled southward until he came to a great, deep river, wide and impassable. How to get across he knew not, for no boat was at hand and the time was too short to make a raft, for behind him were his enemies swiftly pursuing.

In a great strait, he cried out:

"Alas, shall I, the Child of the Sun and the Grandson of the Yellow River, be stopped here powerless by this stream?"

Then as if his father, the Sun, had whispered to him what to do, he drew his bow and shot many arrows here and there into the water, nearly emptying his quiver.

For a few moments nothing happened. To his companions it seemed a waste of good weapons. What would their leader have left to fight his pursuers when they appeared, if his quiver were empty?

But in a moment more the waters appeared to be strangely agitated. Soon they were flecked and foaming. From up and down the stream, and in front of them, the fish were swimming toward East Light, poking their noses out of the water as if they would say:

"Get on our backs and we'll save you." They crowded together in so dense a mass that on their spines a bridge was soon formed, on which men could stand.

"Quick!" shouted East Light to his companions, "let us flee! Behold the king's horsemen coming down the hill after us."

So over the bridge of fish backs, scaly and full of spiny fins, the four young men fled. As soon as they gained the opposite shore, the bridge of fishes dissolved. Yet scarcely had they swum away, when those who were in pursuit had gained the water's edge, on the other side. In vain the king's soldiers shot their arrows to kill East Light and his three companions. The shafts fell short and the river was too deep and wide to swim their horses over. So the four young men escaped safely.

Marching on farther a few miles, East Light met three strange persons who seemed to be awaiting his coming. They welcomed him warmly and invited him to be their king and rule over their city. The first was dressed in seaweed, the second in hempen garments, and the third in embroidered robes. These men represented the three classes of society; first fishermen and hunters; second farmers and artisans; and lastly rulers of the tribes.

So in this land named Fuyu, rich in the five grains, wheat, rice, and millet, bean and sugarcane, the new king was joyfully welcomed by his new subjects. The men were tall, brave and courteous. Besides being good archers, they rode horses skilfully. They ate out of bowls with chop-sticks and used round dishes at their feasts. They wore ornaments of large pearls and jewels of red jade cut and polished.

The Fuyu people gave the fairest virgin in their realm to be the bride of King East Light and she became a gracious queen, greatly beloved of her subjects and many children were born to them.

East Light ruled long and happily. Under his reign the people of Fuyu became civilized and highly prosperous. He taught the proper relations of ruler and ruled and the laws of marriage, besides better methods of cooking and house-building. He also showed them how to dress their hair. He introduced the wearing of the topknot. For thousands of years topknots were the fashion in Fuyu and in Korea.

Hundreds of years after East Light died, and all the tribes and states in the peninsula south of the Everlasting White Mountains wanted to become one nation and one kingdom, they called their country after East Light, but in a more poetical form,- Cho-sen, which means Morning Radiance, or the Land of the Morning Calm.

PRINCE SANDALWOOD, THE FATHER OF KOREA

Four little folks lived in the home of Mr. Kim, two girls and two boys. Their names were Peach Blossom and Pearl, Eight-fold Strength and Dragon. Dragon was the oldest, a boy. Grandma Kim was very fond of telling them stories about the heroes and fairies of their beautiful country.

One evening when Papa Kim came home from his office in the Government buildings, he carried two little books in his hand, which he handed over to Grandma. One was a little almanac looking in its bright cover of red, green and blue as gay as the piles of cakes and confectionery made when people get married; for every one knows how rich in colors are pastry and sweets for the bride's friends at a Korean wedding party.

The second little book contained the direction sent out by the Royal Minister of Ceremonies for the celebration of the festival in honor of the Ancestor-Prince, Old Sandalwood, the Father of Korea. Twice a year in Ping Yang City they made offerings of meat and other food in his honor, but always uncooked.

"Who was old Sandalwood?" asked Peach Blossom, the older of the little girls.

"What did he do?" asked Yongi (Dragon), the older boy.

"Let me tell you," said Grandma, as they cuddled together round her on the oiled-paper carpet over the main flue at the end of the room where it was warmest; for it was early in December and the wind was roaring outside.

"Now I shall tell you, also, why the bear is good and the tiger bad," said Grandma. "Well, to begin-

"Long, long ago, before there were any refined people in the Land of Dawn, and no men but rude savages, a bear and a tiger met together. It was on the southern slope of Old Whitehead Mountain in the forest. These wild animals were not satisfied with the kind of human beings already on the earth, and they wanted better ones. They thought that if they could become human they would be able to improve upon the quality. So these patriotic beasts, the bear and the tiger, agreed to go before Hananim, the Great One of Heaven and Earth, and ask him to change at once their form and nature; or, at least, tell them how it could be done.

"But where to find Him- that was the question. So they put their heads down in token of politeness, stretched out their paws and waited a long while, hoping to get light on the subject.

"Then a Voice spoke out saying, 'Eat a bunch of garlic and stay in a cave for twenty-one days. If you do, you will become human.'

"So into the dark cave they crawled, chewed their garlic and went to sleep.

"It was cold and gloomy in the cave and with nothing to hunt or eat, the tiger got tired. Day after day he moped, snarled, growled and behaved rudely to his companion. But the bear bore the tiger's insults.

"Finally on the eleventh day, the tiger, seeing no signs of losing his stripes or of shedding his hair, claws or tail, and with no prospect of fingers or toes in view, concluded to give up trying to become a man. He bounded out of the cave and at once went hunting in the woods, going back to his old life.

"But the bear, patiently sucking her paw, waited till the twenty-one days had passed. Then her hairy hide and claws dropped off, like an overcoat. Her nose and ears suddenly shortened and she stood upright- a perfect woman.

"Walking out of the cave the new creature sat beside a brook, and in the pure water beheld how lovely she was. There she waited to see what would take place next.

"About this time while these things were going on down in the world matters of interest were happening in the skies. Whanung, the Son of the Great One in the Heavens, asked his father to give him an earthly kingdom to rule over. Pleased with his request, the Lord of Heaven decided to present his son with the Land of the Dragon's Back, which men called Korea.

"Now as everybody knows, this country of ours, the Everlasting Great Land of the Dayspring, rose up on the first morning of creation out of the sea, in the form of a dragon.

His spine, loins and tail form the great range of mountains that makes the backbone of our beautiful country, while his head rises skyward in the eternal White Mountain in the North. On its summit amid the snow and ice lies the blue lake of pure water, from which flow out our boundary rivers."

"What is the name of this lake?" asked Yongi the boy.

"The Dragon's Pool," said Grandma Kim, "and during one whole night, ever so long ago, the dragon breathed hard and long until its breath filled the heavens with clouds. This was the way that the Great One in the Skies prepared the way for his son's coming to earth.

"People thought there was an earthquake, but when they woke up in the morning and looked up to the grand mountain, so gloriously white, they saw the cloud rising far up in the sky. As the bright sun shone upon it, the cloud turned into pink, red, yellow and the whole eastern sky looked so lovely that our country then received its name- the Land of Morning Radiance.

"Down out of his cloud of many colors, and borne on the wind, Whanung, the Heavenly Prince, descended first to the mountain top, and then to the lower earth. When he entered the great forest he found a beautiful woman sitting by the brookside. It was the bear that had been transformed into lovely human shape and nature.

"The Heavenly Prince was delighted. He chose her as his bride and, by and by, a little baby boy was born.

"The mother made for her son a cradle of soft moss and reared her child in the forest.

"Now the people who dwelt at the foot of the mountain were in those days very rude and simple. They wore no hats, had no white clothes, lived in huts, and did not know how to warm their houses with flues running under the floors, nor had they any books or writings. Their sacred place was under a sandalwood tree, on a small mountain named Tabak, in Ping Yang province.

"They had seen the cloud rising from the Dragon's Pool so rich in colors, and as they looked they saw it move southward and nearer to them, until it stood over the sacred sandalwood tree; when out stepped a white-robed being, and descending through the air alighted in the forest and on the tree.

"Oh, how beautiful this spirit looked against the blue sky! Yet the tree was far away and long was the journey to it.

"'Let us all go to the sacred tree,' said the leader of the people. So together they hied over hill and valley until they reached the holy ground and ranged themselves in circles about it.

"A lovely sight greeted their eyes. There sat under the tree a youth of grand appearance, arrayed in princely dress. Though young looking and rosy in face, his countenance was august and majestic. Despite his youth, he was wise and venerable.

"'I have come from my ancestors in Heaven to rule over you, my children,' he said, looking at them most kindly.

"At once the people fell on their knees and all bent reverently, shouting:

"'Thou art our king, we acknowledge thee, and will loyally obey only thee.'

"Seeing that they wanted to know what he could tell them, he began to instruct them, even before he gave them laws and rules and taught them how to improve their houses. He told them stories. The first one explained to them why it was that the bear is good and the tiger bad.

"The people wondered at his wisdom, and henceforth the tiger was hated, while people began to like the bear more and more.

"'What name shall we give our King, so that we may properly address him?' asked the people of their elders. 'It is right that we should call him after the place in which we saw him, under our holy tree. Let his title, therefore, be the August and Venerable Sandalwood.' So they saluted him thus and he accepted the honor.

"Seeing that the people were rough and unkempt, Prince Sandalwood showed them how to tie up and dress their hair. He ordained that men should wear their long locks in the form of a topknot. Boys must braid their hair and let it hang down over their backs. No boy could be called a man, until he married a wife. Then he could twist his hair into a knot, put on a hat, have a head-dress like an adult and wear a long white coat.

"As for the women, they must plait their tresses and wear them plainly at their neck, except at marriage, or on great occasions of ceremony. Then they might pile up their hair like a pagoda and use long hairpins, jewels, silk and flowers.

"Thus our Korean civilization was begun, and to this day the law of the hat and hair distinguishes us above all people," said Grandma. "We still honor the August and Venerable Prince Sandalwood. Now, good-night, my darlings."

THE RABBIT'S EYES

There was trouble down in the fish world under the waves. Indeed, every creature with fins and a tail was in distress, for the king of the fishes was suffering with a dreadful pain in his mouth. It had come about in this way.

One day while swimming around in the waters outside his palace, the king of the fishes saw something hanging in the water that looked as if it were good to eat. So at once His Majesty gulped it down, when, oh horrors! he found he had barely escaped swallowing a fish hook, which stuck fast in his gills. It had been baited by some fishermen up in a boat on the sea top. When the king of the fishes found the dreadful thing in his mouth, he jerked himself away. The line broke but the hook remained, giving the king a fever and much pain.

How to get the iron out and heal His Majesty was now the question. All the wise creatures in the ocean, from the turtle to the gudgeon and from the tittleback to the whale, were summoned to the palace to see what could be done. Many a sage noddle was bent, and eye blinked and fin wagged, as the marine doctors talked the matter over in the council. The turtle was considered the most learned and expert of them all. Many were his feelings of the king's pulse and his looking down into his throat, before Dr. Turtle would pronounce what was the real trouble or write a prescription for his patient. Finally, after consultation with the other doctors that had fins and tails, or were in scales and shell, it was decided that nothing less than a poultice made of rabbits' eyes would loosen the hook and end His Majesty's troubles.

So Dr. Turtle was ordered to go to the seashore and invite a rabbit to come down into the world under the sea, that they might make a poultice of his eyes and apply the warm mess to the king's throat.

Arriving on the sea beach, at the foot of a high hill, Dr. Turtle, looking far up, found Mr. Rabbit out of his burrow and taking a promenade along the edge of the forest. Forthwith Dr. Turtle waddled across the beach and part way up the hill, climbing hard, until he began to puff and blow. He had enough breath left, however, to salute Brother Bunny with a good-morning. Very politely the rabbit returned the greeting.

"It's a hot day," said Dr. Turtle, as he pulled out his handkerchief, wiped his horny forehead, and cleaned the sand out of his claws.

"Yes, but the scenery is so fine, Dr. Turtle, that you must be glad you're out of the water to see such lovely mountains. Don't you think Korea is a fine country? There is no land in the world so beautiful as ours. The mountains, the rivers, the seashore, the forests, the flowers- - "

If Dr. Turtle had let the rabbit run on, praising his own country, he would have forgotten his errand; but, thinking of His Majesty, the suffering fish king, with the cruel hook in his mouth, Dr. Turtle interrupted Bunny, saying:

"Oh, yes, Brother Bunny, this view of the landscape and country is all very beautiful, but it can't compare to the gems and jewels, trees and flowers, sweet odors and everything lovely down in the world under the sea."

At this, the rabbit pricked up his ears. It was all new to him. He had never heard that there was anything under the water but common fishes and seaweed and when these were decayed and washed up along the seashore- well, he had his ideas about them. They did not smell sweet at all. Now he heard a different story. His curiosity was roused. "What you tell me, my friend, is interesting. Go on."

Thereupon Dr. Turtle proceeded to tell of most wonderful mountains and valleys down on the floor of the deep sea, with every kind of rare water plants, red, orange-color, green, blue, white, with trees of gold and silver, besides flowers of every color and delightful perfume.

"You surprise me," said Brother Bunny, getting more interested.

"Yes, and all sorts of good things to eat and drink, with music and dancing, handsome serving maids and everything nice. Come along and be our guest. Our king has sent me to invite you."

"May I go?" asked Brother Bunny, delighted.

"Yes, at once. Get on my back and I'll carry you."

So the rabbit ran and the turtle waddled to the water's edge.

"Now hold fast to my front shell," said Dr. Turtle; "we're going under the water."

Down, down below the blue waves they sank until they arrived at the king's palace. There the rabbit found everything was true, as told by the turtle. The colors, the rich gems were as he had said.

Dr. Turtle introduced Brother Bunny to some of the princes and princesses of the kingdom and these showed their guest the sights and treasures of the palace, while Dr. Turtle attended the council of doctors to announce the success of his errand.

But while Mr. Rabbit was enjoying himself, thinking this was the most wonderful place in the world, he overheard them talking. Then he found out why they had brought him there and shown him such honors. Horrified at the idea of losing his eyes, he determined to save his sight and play the tortoise a smart trick. However, of this he told no one.

So when he was politely informed by the royal executioners that he must give up his eyes to make the king well, Brother Bunny broke out with equally polite regrets:

"Really I am so sorry that His Majesty is ill, and you must excuse me that I cannot help him immediately, for the eyes I have in my head now are not real eyes, but only crystal. I was afraid that sea water would hurt my sight, so I took out my ordinary eyes, buried them in the sand and put on these crystal ones, which I usually wear in very dusty or wet weather."

At this the faces of the royal officers fell. How could they break the news to His Majesty and disappoint him?

Brother Bunny seemed to be really sorry for them and spoke up.

"Oh! don't feel bad about it. If you will allow me to return to the beach, I'll dig them up and return in time for the poultice-making," said the rabbit.

So, getting on Dr. Turtle's back, Brother Bunny was soon out of the water and on land.

In a jiffy he jumped off, scampered away, and reached the woods, showing only his cotton tail. Soon he was out of sight.

Dr. Turtle shed tears and returned to tell how a rabbit had outwitted him.

TOPKNOTS AND CROCKERY HATS

Long, long ago in China, even centuries before the great Confucius was born, there lived a wise and learned man named Kija. He was the chief counselor at court, and all honored him for his justice and goodness. He was always kind to boys and girls.

But when a great war broke out and a new line of rulers came into power, Kija declined to serve the king of the country and resolved to emigrate to the far East. There he would teach the savage people manners and refinement.

The new king was sorry to have Kija go, for he respected his character and wisdom. However he allowed five thousand of the best people, most of them Kija's followers, to accompany their master among the Eastern savages. Many of the common folks wept when they saw the emigrants leave China the flowery country to go into the Eastern wilderness and journey to an unknown region, full of dark swamps and thick forests. Kija was going where there were no roads, farms, or houses, and the woods were full of wild beasts, especially big bears and terrible tigers that liked to feed on human beings. It was even said that there were flying serpents that had wings and leopards that stood up holding lightning in their paws.

Over the great plains of Manchuria, Kija and his army of people, little folks and big ones, marched ever toward the rising sun, until they crossed the Duck Green River, which we call the Yalu. After a few days more, they came to the Great Eastern River (Ta Tong). There the land was very beautiful and Kija resolved to settle and build a city. From the tinted clouds at sunrise, rosy, golden, flushed with every shade of red, and lovely with changing colors the new country had been named Cho-sen, or Land of Morning Radiance. As the sun rose and raced toward the west, where his homeland lay, Kija welcomed the good omen as a double blessing. He saw in the calm of his first day in his adopted country a threefold pledge of continued good-will between the new kingdom and the old empire, Heaven's favoring sign of his loyalty to the Chinese Emperor, and the surety of good-will from the spirit of the Ever White Mountain.

Having laid out for his colony a city which was to be the capital of his kingdom, Kija began to build a wall. He named the city Ping Yang, which means Northern Castle.

"But now that we have safely arrived as after a voyage, the city shall be shaped like a boat," said Kija. "Within its walls no wells shall be dug, lest this, like boring holes, should make the boat sink. Then also, on the outside, to the west, shall stand the rock pillar to which the boat city shall be forever moored."

Kija was ably assisted by his wise men, who were skilled in literature, poetry, music, medicine and philosophy. Together they published eight great laws for the kingdom:

-Agriculture for the men.

-Weaving for the women.

-Punishment of thieves.

-Murderers to be beheaded.

-All land to be divided into nine squares, the central one to be tilled in common for the benefit of the State.

-Simple life for all.

-The law of marriage.

-Wicked people to be made slaves.

Kija laid out roads, established measures and distances and ordained the rules of politeness. He taught the savage people how to build good houses, each with roofs of thatch or tile and a *kang*, or warming place, by means of flues running under the floors. There was a fire at one end and a chimney at the other, so that the smoke came out of the ground half-way up the house wall. Twice a day, at morning and sunset, the people fed with fuel the furnaces or cooking place in the kitchen. Then the flames, heat and smoke passed through the flues, warming the rooms. Thus the houses were made cozy and comfortable. Every day one can see the morning and the evening cloud of the *kang* smoke hanging over the city. It is in these flues and around the cooking pots that Tokgabi, the merry scamp, plays his most mischievous tricks. He is a sooty fellow and loves nothing better than to amuse or plague mortal men.

The people of the land were very rough and savage in these early times and being constantly given to hard fighting, murder was common. So Kija found that he must devise some way to make them peaceable. At first he tried gentle methods. He saw that the rude fellows wore their hair long, letting their locks stream out over their backs and that they were often unkempt and slovenly to the last degree. Besides they hated combs and did not like to get washed.

So Kija republished the law of Dan Kun, the spirit of the mountain, who had two topknots. He ordered that every married man should bind up his hair into a knot, or chignon, on top of his head. Thus the Korean topknot was established by law. As for the younger fellows they must plait their hair and wear it in a braid down their backs. Until a man got a wife, he was only a boy, and must hold his tongue in presence of his elders. If caught wearing a topknot before he had a wife, he was punished severely.

Nevertheless the rough people mistook the good purposes of Kija. They used the topknot as a handle to catch hold of when fighting in the streets. The big, burly fellows pulled the smaller men around most cruelly. Furthermore, they were accustomed to crack each other's skulls with clubs, so that many dead men were found in the streets. To stop these quarrels and murders, Kija invented a hat that would keep brawlers at least a yard apart.

"I'll settle their quarrels for them, once and forever," said Kija. "I'll make their fun cost each man a pretty rope of cash. Every time two bullies fight, they shall have a lot of crockery to pay for."

So Kija caused big heavy hats to be moulded of clay. These measured four feet across and were two feet high, weighing many pounds. These he had baked in ovens until they were hard as stone. They looked like big porridge bowls turned upside down.

Every fellow who had a bad temper, or was known to quarrel was compelled to wear a hat of this heavy earthenware. Whenever a crowd of men-folks got together they looked like a field of moving mushrooms.

When men fought they only cracked their crockery. In this way

Kija easily found out who broke the law so that he could punish them. Then they had to go to the potter's and buy new hats. This made it quite an expensive affair, for a good half year's wages was required to pay for a hat.

Kija's wisdom was justified. The earthenware hats proved to be a good protection to the sacred topknots and the men liked them. Quarrelsome fellows stopped pulling hair and smashing heads. It got to be the custom, instead of punching a man's face or cracking his skull, to let off one's bad temper in scolding and calling names, glaring frightfully, or rolling one's eyes,- all of which of course made no blood flow. The bumpkin who could make the most frightful faces, grind his teeth most savagely, and look more like a devil than the other fellow, was reckoned the bravest and the victor.

Before many months, a street quarrel got to be a perfectly silent battle of ugly faces and terrible gestures. What at first promised to be a bloody murder usually became a noiseless duel, or a quarrel between deaf and dumb folks. This furnished violent exercise for eyes and teeth only, but it passed off like steam out of a kettle. In time a gentleness like a great calm settled over the land.

The crockery hats became all the fashion. They were very popular. Even the women wanted to wear them, because they were so useful. When turned over, they served as wash-bowls and many a good housewife borrowed her husband's second-best hat to do the family washing in. They were useful also for feed troughs and drinking basins for the horses and cattle and for donkeys to eat their beans.

The women, though not permitted to wear crockery bonnets, were pleased with the way Kija treated them. He took the clubs of the rough men, which they no longer needed, and handed them over to the wives and daughters to use in pounding the clothes on wash days and for ironing. In this way, the Korean women learned the wonderful art of putting a fine gloss on the starched clothes of the male members of the family, especially on the long white coat of the house father. Thus by changing sticks that had been used as skull-crackers into starch polishers, Kija changed also ruffians into gentlemen. Ever since, Koreans have been famous for their politeness.

Happily also, the men grew more refined in their manners and were kind to their wives and daughters, because they saw such shining clothes. When hot weather came and the gentlemen complained of the heat, and fearing that perspiration might spoil their fine clothes, Kija allowed them to make inside suits of bamboo sticks, as fine as thread or wire. Thus the Korean gentleman wore his outer clothes on a frame hung from his shoulders like a hooped skirt. It seemed like taking off one's flesh and sitting in his bones thus to wear bamboo underclothes.

By and by, as manners improved, finding garments thus made from the cane-brake so comfortable, the men gave up their heavy crockery hats. In place of these they wore "bird cages" made of horsehair over their topknots, and out-of-doors put on "roofs" of straw, reed, basket-ware, or shining black lacquered paper, according to their rank in society. Thus it came to pass that Korea is the land of hats.

FANCHA AND THE MAGPIE

A thousand years ago or more, there was a tribe in the cold and desert land of the Tartars, north of Korea, which grew to be famous in that part of the world. The men let their hair grow long and then plaited it into a long braid that hung down their backs, but they shaved the front of their heads. These people were called Manchus.

Almost from babyhood they were trained to ride on horses, and in time they became such bold horsemen and warriors, that they swooped down in thousands like clouds from their mountain land into warmer and richer regions. They had terrible bows and arrows, spears and swords, and they won many victories, so that other tribes joined them. They captured great China and invaded Korea.

As long as they had been wandering tribes in the desert, they were poor and lived on plain food that the grassy plains and forests could furnish, such as nuts, herbs, the milk of mares, and mutton. Their clothes were made of the wool from their own sheep. They were not proud, except of their strength, and they never asked who their grandfathers were.

But it was very different when they came to be rulers of a vast empire, rich and great like China, which had books and writing and a history of thousands of years. The elegant Chinese gentlemen and nobles used to call their conquerors the "horsey Tartars." So they learned to wash and perfume themselves, and to care for jade, and tea, and porcelain, and silk, and other things Chinese.

Now it came to pass that when these people out of the desert sat on the thrones, and wore crowns on their heads, and dressed in satin, with jeweled robes and velvet shoes, they wanted to know who had been their ancestors long ago, and whence they came.

It would not do to believe that the fathers and mothers of so mighty a race were once common folks who in the distant deserts lived on acorns and pine nuts, with horse meat often, and mutton occasionally, and mare's milk for dessert, or that they dressed in sheep skin and tended horses like stable boys.

Oh no! If the common folks, whom they now governed and made obey them, knew that the nobles who now lived in Peking and bullied the Koreans were once only stable and butcher boys, and had no houses but lived only in tents, there would surely be trouble. These Koreans and Chinese might disobey and rebel. They might even cut off their pigtails, which the Tartars had forced them to wear, and clip their locks, like men in Europe and America. These white-faced and bearded foreigners they called "Southern Barbarians," because their ships came up from the south by way of India.

"What shall we do to make the Chinese and Koreans think we are somebody?" asked the Chinese Emperor of his wise men.

In the council it was the custom to ask first the younger men to tell what they thought about it, and for the oldest and wisest to speak last. They talked over the matter a long time. Finally one graybeard took off his goggles and made answer. He had on his nose a pair of horn-rimmed green glasses, bigger than those which anyone else wore. These it was supposed enabled him to look farther into the past and the future than his fellows. For the bigger the goggles, the more learned a man was supposed to be. He looked as wise as a stuffed owl, and was very fat. He spoke last, after all the younger counselors had been invited to give their opinions. Behind his back they called him Green Lamps, because of his goggles and their color.

Now in Korea and China it is not polite to keep your spectacles on your nose, when you look into the face of any person to whom you are talking. So pulling off his goggles old Green Lamps got down on his knees. Then he performed the kow-tow. That was done by knocking the matting of the floor with his forehead nine times. Green Lamps nearly broke his stiff bones in doing it, and then he addressed the Emperor, whose title was the Son of Heaven, as follows:

"Sire, the common people will not respect us unless we can show that our far-off ancestors were not born like plain folks, but came down from Heaven. There is an old woman, nearly two cycles or one hundred and seventeen years old, who tells the children about our distant forebears, who dropped out of the sky. Shall I call her in?"

"What is her name?" inquired His Imperial Majesty.

"Mrs. Crinkles, they call her, O Son of Heaven," answered Green Lamps.

"Summon her before me instantly," said the Emperor, and he waved his lotus-bud sceptre.

Now Green Lamps was a foxy old fellow. He wanted to get even higher in the Emperor's favor and had expected this. So, having the old lady ready in another room of the palace, he went out and brought her in. She was all ready to tell her story, with which she had interested the children for a long time. It was the same story which her grandmother had told, when around the fire on winter nights young and old gathered to hear, while the winds howled and the snow covered the land. Once, Mrs. Crinkles was a rosy maid, but now in Peking she was the oldest living person among the Tartars.

The young women called her Mrs. Crinkles because of her face which was so wrinkled and puckered. Once while the old lady was telling her story a mischievous maiden started to count how many wrinkles and puckers, the old lady had in her face, but after reaching seventy-four she stopped, for fear there might be one pucker for every year; and the number for some reason was thought to be unlucky.

In hobbled Mrs. Crinkles. She was already bowed with the weight of years so that when she bowed still lower the court chamberlain, remarking that it beat the kow-tow itself, excused her from making the nine prostrations of her stiff old bones. In fact it was feared that if she got down, she could never get up again. So she was allowed to sit and begin her story.

Her speech was not in the polished Chinese tongue, which for ages since Confucius has been refined by poets and scholars and literary ladies and gentlemen, but was in plain Tartar, or Manchu. Yet the general style of her narrative was very fine. As the old lady told it with animation and fine gestures all eyes sparkled and the Emperor's visage- they called it the Dragon Countenance- beamed with delight.

This was the narrative:

On the other side of the Ever White Mountains, which divide Korea from Manchuria, is the Land of Lakes. On one of these, as in a mirror, the glorious blue sky and the forms of the snow-covered, majestic mountains are reflected. At night when the stars come out the waveless mirror is spangled with jewels. The fame of this crystal clear flood and the lovely tints which the sunrise and sunset daily made upon it reached even to the skies. There were three lovely virgins who dwelt in the Heavenly palaces and they wanted to come down and bathe in the water of this lake and live on its shores.

Permission was given them by the Lord of Heaven, and descending to the earth they were as happy as fairies could be. They never tired of their enjoyment, seeing their own beautiful faces in the mirror of the lake. When they rose early in the morning, to see the golden sun rise and tint the clouds and waters, it seemed like music when song answered song. When the light breezes rippled the surface of the lake they clapped their hands with delight and at bedtime they were lulled to sleep by the waves lapping on the quiet shore.

They fell in love with the beautiful land and became so charmed with it that in time they forgot about their old home and never wished to go back again into the skies. They were very kind to all living things and especially to the magpies. These feathered creatures were very plentiful and tame, so the maidens made pets of them and chose the magpie as their sacred bird.

Fond of gazing into the blue above and bathing in the liquid blue beneath, the three sisters went often into the lake. Leaving their robes on the pebbly beach, the youngest one always stepped last into the crystal waters. One day they noticed a magpie flying far above them in the air, which seemed to motion as if it had a message to deliver. On coming near they saw that it bore in its bill a blood-red fruit. Descending near where their clothes lay on the beach it poised for a moment, and then dropped the red fruit on the garment of the youngest of the sisters.

Rushing out of the water they sat down to talk over the wonderful incident. Then they agreed that this gift of the bird, which was sacred in their eyes, was a happy omen and meant that something good was to follow, though the magpie, after circling around their heads, flew away. They divided the fruit, which had a most delicious taste, enjoying it also as a message from Heaven.

From this divine token brought by a magpie, the sacred bird, the youngest of the virgins conceived and bore a son. They named the baby boy Golden Family Stem, for they felt sure that he would grow up and become the founder of a dynasty of kings, who should take the name of Great Bright from the shining water near which he was born.

The young mother brought up her boy to believe that he was not like ordinary mortals but was Heaven-born, and therefore should be noble in all his actions. When he grew up he was to be a prince of peace healing the quarrels of men, which should bring happiness and prosperity to them and to all the world.

So in the shadow of the great mountains, which were so high that they seemed to touch the sky and were as the shadows of the eternal world itself, he grew up. Nothing did he love more than to watch the play of light and shade on these mountain sides and in the valleys, as well as in the reflections on the fair face of the lake. These were to him as the smile of the Great Guardian Spirit.

But by and by his dear mother's breath ceased and she "entered into the icy caves of the dead," and he found himself an orphan with no one near him; for long since the other two virgins had gone away he knew not where.

Left alone instead of staying among the mountains the boy resolved to take the name of Fancha, or Heaven-born, and to go out into the world and lead men.

He at once set about to build a boat and in this, when finished, he floated down the outlet of the lake into a river. It happened that he landed at a place where three tribes or clans were at war, each one with the other. They were rude enough fellows, accustomed to brawls, and they cared nothing about other common fellows who were like themselves and no better.

But when they saw this noble youth alone and unarmed step fearlessly over the gunwale of the boat and advance to meet them in a friendly way, they were mightily impressed at his noble appearance and his courage in coming among them. When he told them the story of his birth, and that his mother had called him her Heaven-born son, they one and all shouted "Our chief!" and put on him the signs and tokens of lordship over them.

At once the Heaven-born youth became a great leader. At the head of his brave warriors he was always victorious, but he never provoked war. Other tribes flocked to his standard and in time he built a city, and for his wife and queen married a princess in the principal tribe, the daughter of a great chief, and several sons were born in his home.

But wars continued, for the custom of fighting was too old to be given up at once. In one of the battles he and all his sons except one, who was named Fancha, were killed. This one was chased by the enemy for a long distance over the open plains; for they hoped to capture him and make him their prisoner, before he could get into the forest and hide.

But when Fancha reached a dense dark wood a deliverer came to him in the form of the sacred bird, the magpie. This creature settled on his head, and Fancha at once took it to be the token of safety and to have been sent from Heaven.

When his pursuers rushed into the forest and began their glances among the trees looking around for the lad's hiding place, he stood as still as a post. They seeing the bird supposed the figure was a piece of dried wood or the splinter of a tree struck by lightning, and rushed on and past him. By and by they gave up the hunt: by which time, Fancha had escaped to a place of safety.

"The rest of the story Your Majesty knows," concluded the old lady, "for Fancha was your ancestor of seventeen generations ago."

The great Emperor of all the Chinas was intensely interested and deeply moved at the story of the aged woman, and he loaded her with presents and honors, and created for her the office of Chief Story-Teller to the Imperial children. Besides this he made provision for her comfort as long as she lived. With a vermilion pencil he wrote with his own hand the order that when she "ascended to the skies" she should be buried in a gilded sandal-wood coffin, receive a state funeral, have a marble tablet over her grave, and be awarded posthumous honors.

As for old Green Lamps he was raised one degree higher in office, given the honors of wearing a jade button on his cap, and the right to ride in his palanquin nearer the Imperial palace door than any other mandarin, except the prime minister.

THE SNEEZING COLOSSUS

Mr. Kim, who lived at the foot of the mountains, was a lazy lout. He had a family to support, but he did not like steady work. He preferred to smoke his pipe- as long as a yardstick- and to wait for something to turn up.

One day, his wife, tired of trying to feed hungry children from empty dishes, gave her husband a good scolding and bade him begone and get something for the household. This consisted of father, mother, and four little folks, whose faces were not often washed, besides a little dog. This puppy, when danger was near, always ran into the house through a little square hole cut in the door, and when safely within barked lustily.

So Mr. Kim went out to the mountains to find something- a root of ginseng, a nugget of gold, or some precious stone, perhaps, if he were lucky. If not, some berries, wild grapes or pears might do. Meanwhile at home, his wife pounded the grain that was left in the larder for the children's dinner.

Mr. Kim rambled over the rocks a long time without seeing anything worth carrying away. When it was about noon he came to one of the mighty mir-yeks, or colossal stone Buddhas, cut out of the solid mountain. It rose in the air many yards high. Ages ago in the days of Buddhism, when monasteries covered the land and Buddhist friars and nuns chanted Sanscrit hymns to the praise of Lord Buddha, devout men, laboring many months, chiseled this towering colossus into human form. Its nose stood out three feet, its mouth was four feet wide. On its flat head was a cap, made of a slab of granite and shaped like a student's mortar-board, on which ten men could stand without crowding one another.

Long gone and forgotten were the monks, and the monastery had fallen to ruins. The forest had grown up around the great stone image until it was nearly hidden by the tall trees surrounding it. In front, from the ground up, the wild grape-vines had gripped the stone with their tendrils and spread their matted branches and greenery until they nearly covered the image up to its neck.

But out of a crevice in the head of the figure grew a pear tree, sprung from a seed dropped long ago by the great-grandfather of one of the birds singing and chirping near by. And, oh joy! at the end of the outer branch was growing a ripe, luscious pear nearly as big as a man's head. What a prize! It would, when cut up, make a dessert for the whole family. Happy Kim! He blessed his lucky star.

Seizing hold of the bushes and wild grape-vines, by dint of great effort Mr. Kim climbed upward and got as far as the chin of the great stone face. Above him protruded the big nose, the nostrils of which gaped like caverns. Yet although he was standing with his foot on the stone lips and holding on to the nose, despite all his exertions, he could get no further up the granite face. He was at his wit's end. Far above hung the delicious looking pear as if to tantalize him. A gentle breeze was swaying the fruit to and fro, and it seemed to say, "Take me if you can."

But the nose, being polished, was slippery and the ears were too smooth to climb. What could he take hold of? Surely to shin up any further was impossible. Must he give up the pear?

A bright thought entered his head. He would crawl up into the right nostril and hope for an exit to the top. So, thinking he might find his way he began like an insect to enter the hole and soon the man Kim disappeared from sight, as with hands and feet he climbed into the darkness.

Wasn't it dangerous to tickle the nostrils of the great stone man in this way?

But whatever Kim may have thought he kept on, determined to get that pear, come what might.

Suddenly a blast loud enough to rend the mountain was heard. *Hash-ho!* Had an earthquake or tempest taken place? Was this rolling thunder?

No, the colossus had sneezed. Thus the stone man got rid of the intruder. The first thing Mr. Kim knew, he was flying through the air, and he tumbled upon the bushes. His wits were gone. He knew nothing. This was about one o'clock in the afternoon.

Mr. Kim lay asleep or unconscious till near sun-down. Then he woke up and realized what had happened. There was the stone nose beetling over him far up toward the sky.

But in sneezing so hard, the colossus had shaken its head also and the big pear had dropped off. Kim found it lying by his side, and picking it up went on his way rejoicing.

At home the little dog looking through the square hole saw him, barked welcome, and a right merry supper they had over the big pear cut into slices, as Mr. Kim told the story of his adventures.

A BRIDEGROOM FOR MISS MOLE

By the river Kingin stands the great stone image, or Miryek, that was cut out of the solid rock ages ago. Its base lies far beneath the ground and around its granite cap many feet square the storm-clouds gather and play as they roll down the mountain.

Down under the earth near this mighty colossus lived a soft-furred mole and his wife. One day a daughter was born to them. It was the most wonderful mole baby that ever was known. The father was so proud of his lovely offspring that he determined to marry her only to the grandest thing in the whole universe. Nothing else would satisfy his pride in the beautiful creature he called his own.

Father Mole sought long and hard to find out where and what, in all nature, was considered the most wonderful. He called in his neighbors and talked over the matter with them. Then he visited the king of the moles and asked the wise ones in his court to decide for him. One and all agreed that the Great Blue Sky was above everything else in glory and greatness.

So up to the Sky the Mole Father went and offered his daughter to be the bride of the Great Blue, telling how with his vast azure robe the Sky had the reputation, both on the earth and under it, of being the greatest thing in the universe.

But much to the Mole Father's surprise, the Sky declined.

"No, I am not the greatest. I must refer you to the Sun. He controls me, for he can make it day or night as he pleases. Only when he rises can I wear my bright colors. When he goes down darkness covers the world and men do not see me at all, but the stars instead. Better take your charming daughter to him."

So to the Sun went Mr. Mole and though afraid to look directly into his face, he made his plea. He would have the Sun marry his attractive daughter.

But the mighty luminary, that usually seemed so fierce, dazzling men's eyesight and able to burn up the grass of the field, seemed suddenly very modest. Instead of accepting at once the offer, the Sun said to the father:

"Alas! I am not master. The Cloud is greater than I, for he is able to cover me up and make me invisible for days and weeks. I am not as powerful as you think me to be. Let me advise you to offer your daughter to the Cloud."

Surprised at this, the Mole Father looked quite disappointed.

Now he was in doubt as to what time he had best propose to the Cloud,- when it was silvery white and glistening in a summer afternoon, or when it was black and threatening a tempest. However, his ambition to get for his daughter the mightiest possible bridegroom prompted him to wait until the lightnings flashed and the thunder rolled. Then appearing before the terrible dark Cloud that shot out fire, he told of the charms of his wonderful daughter and offered her as bride.

"But why do you come to me?" asked the Cloud, its face inky black with the wrath of a storm and its eyes red with the fires of lightning.

"Because you are not only the greatest thing in the universe, but you have proved it by your terrible power," replied the Father Mole.

At this the Cloud ceased its rolling, stopped its fire and thunder and almost laughed.

"So far from being the greatest thing in the world, I am not even my own master. See already how the wind is driving me. Soon I shall be invisible, dissolved in air. Let me commend you to the Wind. The Master of the Cloud will make a grand son-in-law."

Thereupon Papa Mole waited until the Wind calmed down, after blowing away the clouds. Then telling of his daughter's accomplishments and loveliness, he made proffer of his only child as bride to the Wind.

But the Wind was not half so proud as the Mole Father had expected to find him. Very modest, almost bashful seemed the Wind, as he confessed that before Miryek, the colossal stone image, his power was naught.

"Why, I smite that Great Stone Face and its eyes do not even blink. I roar in his ears, but he minds it not. I try to make him sneeze, but he will not. Smite him as I may, he still stands unmoved and smiling. Alas, no. I am not the grandest thing in the universe, while Miryek stands. Go to him. He alone is worthy to marry your daughter."

By this time the Mole Father was not only footsore and weary, but much discouraged also. Evidently all appreciated his shining daughter; but would he be able, after all, to get her a worthy husband?

He rested himself a while and then proceeded to Miryek, the colossus of granite as large as a lighthouse, its head far up in the air, but with ears ready to hear.

The Mole Father squeaked out compliments to the image as being by common confession the greatest thing on earth. He presented his request for a son-in-law and then in detail mentioned the accomplishments of his daughter, sounding her praise at great length. Indeed, he almost ruined his case by talking so long.

With stony patience Miryek listened to the proud father with a twinkle in his white granite eyes. When his lips moved, he was heard to say:

"Fond Parent, what you say is true. I am great. I care not for the sky day or night, for I remain the same in daylight and darkness. I fear not the sun, that cannot melt me, nor the frost that is not able to make me crumble. Cold or hot, in summer or in winter time, I remain unchanged. The clouds come and go, but they cannot move me. Their fire and noise, lightning and thunder, I fear not. Yes, I am great." Then the stone lips closed again.

"You will make, then, a good bridegroom for my daughter? You will marry her, I understand?" asked the proud father as his hopes began to rise, though he was still doubtful.

"I would gladly do so, if I were greatest. But I am not," said Miryek. "Down under my feet is the Mole. He digs with his shovellike hands and makes burrows day and night. His might I cannot resist. Soon he shall undermine my base and I shall topple down and lie like common stone along the earth. Yes! by universal confession, the Mole is the greatest thing in the universe and to him I yield. Better marry your daughter to him."

So after all his journeying, the father sought no further. Advised on all sides, and opinion being unanimous, he found out that the Mole was the greatest thing in the universe. His daughter's bridegroom was found at home and of the same family of creatures. He married her to a young and handsome Mole, and great was the joy and rejoicing at the wedding. The pair were well-mated and lived happily ever afterward.

OLD WHITE WHISKERS AND MR. BUNNY

White Whiskers was the name of a huge, tawny tiger that lived in the mountains of Kang Wen. He was the proudest tiger in the whole peninsula of Korea. He had the most fiery eyes, the longest tail, the sharpest claws, and the widest stripes of any animal in the mountains. He could pull down a cow, fight all the dogs in any village, eat up a man, and was not afraid of a hunter, unless the man carried a gun. As for calves and pigs, he considered them mere tidbits. He could claw off the roof or break the bars of stables where cattle were kept, devour one pig on the spot, and then, slinging another on his back, could trot off to his lair miles away, to give his cubs their dinner of fresh pork.

White Whiskers was especially proud, because he was the retainer of the great genii of the mountains, that men feared and worshiped and in whose honor they built shrines. One of these Mountain Spirits, when he wanted to, could call together all the tigers in his domain, and then, sitting astride the back of the biggest, he would ride off on the clouds or to victory over Korea's enemies. Both tigers and leopards were his messengers to do his bidding. Only the big and swift and striped tigers were chosen to carry out the Mountain Spirit's orders.

One particular matter of business confided to White Whiskers, the great striped tiger, was to visit daily the shrines in the hill passes to see if offerings were continually made. The people who were in terror of both the Mountain Spirit and his servants the tigers, daily offered sacrifice out of fear. They piled up stone, rags, bits of metal, or laid food on dishes for the Mountain Spirit who was very exacting and tyrannical. The poor folks thought that if they did not thus heap up their offerings the spirit would be angry and send the tigers at night to prowl around the village, scratch at their doors, and eat up donkeys, cows, calves, pigs, and even men, women and children. Then the hunters would go out with matchlocks to slay the man eaters, but by this time, in daylight, the tigers were far up into their lairs in the mountain.

Indeed, it was so hard to get a shot at a tiger that the Chinese, who like to make fun of their neighbors in white coats, declared that during one half of the year the Koreans hunt the tigers, and during the other half the tigers hunt the Koreans. That is, the men go out with their guns in summer; but in winter, when men keep within doors, the hungry wild beasts descend from the mountains for their prey.

Now Old White Whiskers was both proud and crafty. For many years he had eaten up pigs, calves, dogs, donkeys and chickens and had twice feasted on men, besides avoiding all their traps and dodging every one of their bullets. So he began to think he could laugh at all his enemies. Yet, proud as he was, he was destined to be outwitted by a creature without strength or sting, claws or hoofs, as we shall see.

Mr. Rabbit, who burrowed in a hill near the village, had often heard the squealing of unfortunate pigs and the kicking of braying donkeys, as they made dinners for Old White Whiskers. Thus far, however, by being very cautious, he had kept out of the striped tyrant's way and maw. But one cold winter's day, coming home, tired, weak and hungry, from having no food since yesterday, just as he was crossing a river on the ice, he met Old White Whiskers face to face. From behind a rock by the shore, near Mr. Bunny's burrow, the big tiger leaped out and tried to freeze the rabbit with terror, by staring at him with his great green eyes. Mr. Bunny knew only too well that tigers love to maul and play with their prey before eating it up, and he thought his last hour had come.

Nevertheless Mr. Bunny was perfectly cool. He did not shiver a bit. He had long expected such a meeting and was ready for Old White Whiskers, intending to throw him off his guard.

Fully expecting, in a minute or two, to tear off the little animal's fur and grind his bones for a dinner, the tiger said to the rabbit:

"I'm hungry. I shall eat you up at once."

"Oh, why should you bother with me?" said Mr. Bunny. "I'm so little and skinny as hardly to make a mouthful for Your Majesty. Just listen to me and I'll get you a royal dinner. I'll go up the mountain and drive the game to your very paws. Only you must do exactly what I tell you."

At this prospect of a full dinner, the tiger actually grinned with delight. The way he yawned, showing his red, cavernous mouth, huge white teeth, each as big as a spike, and the manner of his rolling out his long curved tongue, full of rough points like thorns, nearly scared Mr. Bunny out of his wits. The rabbit had never looked down a tiger's mouth before, but he did not let on that he was afraid. It was only the tiger's way of showing how happy he was, when his mouth watered, and he licked his chops in anticipation of a mighty feast.

"I'll do just as you say," said Old White Whiskers to Mr. Bunny, seeing how grateful the rabbit was to have his own life spared.

"It is my ambition to serve the lord of the mountains," said Mr. Bunny. "So, lie down on the ice here, shut your eyes and do not stir. Now mind you keep your peepers closed, or the charm will fail. I'll make a circle of dry grass and then go round and round you, driving the game to you. If you hear a noise and even some crackling, don't open your eyes till I give you the word. 'Twill take some time."

Old White Whiskers, tired of tramping in the forest and prowling around pig-pens all day but getting nothing, was both hungry and tired. So he resolved, while waiting, to take a good nap. As quickly as one can blow out a candle, he was asleep.

Thereupon Mr. Bunny made himself busy in pulling up all the dry grass he could find and piling it around and close up to Old White Whiskers. Delighted to hear the big brute snoring, he kept on until he had a thick ring of combustibles. Then he set it on fire, waiting till it blazed up high. Then he scampered off to see the fun.

Old White Whiskers, awakened by the crackling, yawned and rubbed his eyes with his paws, wondering what the noise could be.

"Hold on!" screamed Mr. Bunny, "keep your promise," and farther he ran away up the hill.

"Rascal!" growled the tiger as the red tongues of flame leaped up all around him. He had to jump high to escape from the flames with his life. Even as it was, one paw was scorched so that he limped, and his fur was singed so badly that all his long hair and fine looks were gone. When he got back home, the other tigers laughed at him.

Henceforth he had to take second place, for the great Mountain Spirit no longer trusted such a stupid servant.

THE KING OF THE FLOWERS

Korea is the land of beautiful scenery and lovely flowers. Snow white and ruby red are their chief colors. In the spring time when the ice has melted and the rivers have poured their floods into the sea, the whole country blushes with the pink bloom of azaleas. The glens are white with lilies of the valley. The breezes as they sweep the land come laden with perfume.

The girls mark the season of the year and the time of the month by the blossoms even more than by the almanac, for they keep in mind the calendar of the flowers. Daughters that are especially beloved of their parents are named from the blossoms, and the Korean house-father, when affectionate, speaks of his wife as the plum tree. An old song says: The homesick husband, long away from his dear ones, inquires of a fellow townsman newly arrived:

> "'Have you seen my native land?
> Come tell me all you know;
> Did just before the old home door
> The plum tree blossoms show?'"

And the stranger answers promptly:

> "'They were in bloom, though pale, 'tis true,
> And sad, from waiting long for you.'"

This is like the Scotsman who calls his wife his "bonnie briar bush," for in the Land of Morning Glow, they have a language of flowers. Each plant and blossom has a meaning and either delightful or disagreeable associations. It is a compliment to speak of a girl as a pear blossom, for the pear is one of the most glorious of trees and its blooms are lovely to behold. It would hardly do, however, to call her a cinnamon rose, for this flower has evil associations. The gee-sang, as the Koreans pronounce the name of the gei-sha, as the Japanese call the dancing girls, are associated with the cinnamon rose, for did not the sages tell this story?

Twelve centuries ago lived the renowned scholar Sul Chong, the greatest of all the learned men of Korea. His head was as full of knowledge as a persimmon is of pulp, and his ideas were as numerous as the seeds in a pomegranate. He taught his countrymen all that was in the books of China, and in the temple of Confucius his portrait hangs to this day. He lived in the kingdom of Silla, in the days of its glory, when ships from Japan and China sailed into its seaports and the Arabs from Bagdad brought their pretty wares to exchange for gold, ginseng, camphor, porcelain, cinnamon, ginger and tiger skins, to take to their renowned Caliph and his turbaned nobles at court, of whom we read in the "Arabian Nights."

When the King of Silla, Sin Mun, was living in luxury and filling his palace with too many pretty dancing girls, who distracted his mind from attending properly to the affairs of state, Sul Chong **warned his master against the increasing influence of these women by telling him the following story:**

Once upon a time, in spring, the Peony, king of the flowers, blossomed so gorgeously that it became the admiration of all the lovers of beauty in the whole country. Hundreds of people made long journeys to the capital of Silla to see the bright blossoms. In the king's gardens, on very tall stalks, the many branches were heavily laden with large red flowers. These were indeed lovely to behold, but the king of the whole garden was a single peony, grown on one stem, so that all the strength and nourishment of the plant were concentrated in that unique royal bloom. All saluted this flower as king.

When all the other flowers heard of their king's glory, they came to pay their respects at the floral court, of which the Peony was sovereign. All the trees sent their choicest blooms as envoys. In one glorious procession of perfume and color the Peach, Plum, Pear, Apple, and Persimmon trooped in, each making its obeisance to the monarch of all flowers. All these tree blossoms prided themselves on their being so useful to man as harbingers of the delicious fruits to come.

Then, among the bright throng appeared sprightly young virgin flowers, the Tea-Rose, in pearl-tinted frock; the Azalea, in pink; the Lily, in white; the Strawberry Blossom; and a score of other pretty creatures of the garden. Last of all appeared the Cinnamon Rose. She tripped nimbly along in a green skirt and red jacket, with haughty air and breath of spice.

One after the other they were presented to King Peony, and gracefully made their salute. But of them all, the king seemed most to favor Miss Cinnamon Flower. He let the others pass out from the Court, but lingered long with the spicy visitor, spending much time in her society, as if smitten with her charms. By and by he invited Miss Cinnamon Rose to come and live in the palace, and leaving his ministers to carry on the government, he spent all his time in her society. She was installed in a place near His Majesty and seemed always to have his ear and attention, even when the king's prime minister had to wait long for an audience, or even a word. Miss Cinnamon Rose seemed to be the real ruler instead of the king himself.

But one day there came to the palace the flower called Old Man. He looked exactly like an aged beggar dressed in sackcloth and leaning on a staff. Respectfully bowing, he asked if he might share the hospitality of the king's palace. He was welcomed and fed, partaking of the royal bounty. When at last he was given audience of King Peony, and was invited to speak, he said:

"Out along the road, Your Majesty, I heard of your rich feast and good things to eat. Now I hear that you need medicine. Although you dress in Chinese silk and none are equal to you in the magnificence of your robes and the splendor of your Court, yet you are much like me in your wants, and you need a common knife string, as well as I. Is it not so?"

"You are quite right, Old Man," replied the king. "Yet I like this Cinnamon Rose and want her with me. I cannot do without her."

"Yes, Your Majesty. Yet, is it not true that if you keep company with the wise and prudent, your reign will be long, powerful and glorious? But if you consort with the foolish your house will fall? Did not three dynasties of the emperors of Great China fall because of the beautiful women who tempted their Majesties to forget their duties? If it were so with the ancients, how much more so is it now?"

The king blushed, even to a deep crimson. He confessed his faults and reformed his life.

It is said the lesson was not lost on the real human king. He dismissed his harem, sent away the dancing girls and ruled wisely till the day of his death.

TOKGABI'S MENAGERIE

(*Cats and Dogs*)

There are many dogs, but few cats, in Korea. Nobody loves poor pussy there. They are not made pets and are rarely seen in the houses of the people. Even bull calves are more caressed by the children than are cats, and the puppy dog takes the place of Tabby or Grimalkin.

Korean cats are not bob-tailed, like their cousins in Japan; nor is pussy ever used, as the Chinese kitten is, to tell the time of day by the width of the slits in its green eyes.

Alas! the cats in Korea are too wild to enjoy the society of human beings, or human beings theirs! The presence of dogs is especially hateful to them. Mother cats tell their kittens wonderful stories of the cruelty of dogs and why cats and dogs do not agree.

The native roof-scramblers can howl and caterwaul, arch their backs, blow up their tails, spit and scratch, or purr pleasantly, lick their fur, and wash their faces with their paws like cats in other countries. They are highly accomplished as mouse catchers and bird-eaters. Yet they have a hard time of it, for there are too many dogs to make a kitty's life either easy or agreeable. The Korean cat hates to get its feet wet, yet it is often obliged to wade in the water to get rid of the dogs that chase it. As for the furry, purry kittens, one wonders how they ever escape the fierce dogs and grow up at all.

Yet it all came about because a certain cat-ancestor laughed when it shouldn't have done so. Although it was a lot of school-children that made Kitty laugh, the dog never forgave the cat for its frivolity. And this is how it happened.

Long, long ago, one of the mountain fairies had come down into the land from the high peaks, and being kindly treated by an old man named Tip Pul, who kept a wine shop, called Tokgabi and bade him reward the old fellow with a precious stone.

So, one night, Tokgabi dropped the gem into Tip Pul's long-necked wine bottle. Strangely enough, after this, the wine never

ceased. The bottle was always full. Every day Tip Pul sold plenty to his neighbors and it was good and cheap, so that the shopkeeper was very popular. Yet, without any refilling, the flask was always ready to overflow. So Tip Pul had no fear of poverty in extreme old age. Having neither wife nor children, his only companions were a dog named Su Nap, or Snap, for short, and a cat named Mee Yow. All three lived happily together in these times of long ago.

But one day the bottle was found to be empty, and when Tip Pul shook it, nothing rattled inside. Somehow the magic stone had disappeared. Poverty now seemed certain. The old man was nearly paralyzed with grief and his neighbors all came in to sympathize with him. They knew well that they could buy no wine anywhere else so good and so cheap as they had long enjoyed at Tip Pul's shop by the river.

Yet this loss of the wonderful stone was the very making of Tip Pul's pets. As for the cat, she became the most industrious kitty ever known. She at once began to ransack every rat's quarters known, not only in her master's home, but in every house in the village, in search of the missing stone. The racket which that cat kept up at night, among the rafters and beams under the roof, nearly drove some people crazy. They declared that Tokgabi had got drunk by tasting Tip Pul's drams. Yet it was Mee Yow all the time. The cat knocked over tobacco boxes, scratched among hat covers hung on the wall, tipped up the hanging shelves and upset the crockery in the closet over the kitchen stove. In a word, this four-footed creature played every kind of mischief that people usually ascribe to Tokgabi, the sooty imp.

Yet, when any one climbed up to the attic, looked among the rafters, and peered into the darkness, all he could see was a pair of green eyes that shone like the moon. Poking the uncanny thing with fishing poles, or throwing shoes or sticks at it, only caused spitting or snarling. So they knew it was a cat, and not Tokgabi, and betook themselves to bed again. Laying their topknots on their wooden pillows and their bodies on their oiled-paper carpet, they soon fell asleep again. The Koreans do not swear, but the way some good folks hurled bad words on all the ancestors of that cat, clear back to the time of Kija, was dreadful to think of. Indeed, some of their remarks are still preserved in tradition and proverbs. Nevertheless, with all his pains taken, Mee Yow could not find the magic wine-stone. As for Tip Pul, he got poorer and poorer.

The dog could not climb like Puss among the rafters and the roofs, but being able to run fast and having a nose that could smell a tiger a mile off, he made excursions all over the country, even crossing the ice of the frozen river. Although he fought many another dog, chased many a rat into its hole, and worried about a hundred cats, even jumping into wood-sheds and running in and out among the cows and horses, he found nothing. Once, while in a stall where the pony, tied up with a belly-band by ropes to the ceiling, was enjoying its supper of bean soup, the poor dog was nearly kicked to death. The vicious brute, thinking that Snap was trying to steal some beans from its feed box, gave the dog a blow with its hoofs that made Snap go on three legs for a week afterward.

The long winter passed away and the ice melted, but the river water was still cold. One day Pussy, while chasing a rat among the rafters of a house of a Yang-ban or gentleman, brushed its whiskers against a greenish soapstone box, such as the king often sends as a present to those whom he likes. Recognizing the smell of something inside as that of his master's long-lost gem, he tried hard by tooth and claw to open it.

All Pussy's scratching, biting and clawing, however, were in vain. Nor could the dog help in the least. So a bargain was struck with the rats to gnaw open the box and get the magic stone. Both Su Nap and Mee Yow promised to let all rats and mice entirely alone for six months, if one of them would agree to gnaw open the box.

Delighted at the prospect of peace and quiet for half a year, and especially while the grain should be ripening, both rats and mice worked together, until out of a hole gnawed in the box, polished and hard on their teeth as it was, they got the magic stone. Carrying it in their paws, they dropped it where their former enemies, now so peaceful, could get it. At once the dog took the gem in his mouth and ran to the river, Mee Yow following after.

"Now, Kit," said Snap, "get on my back and hold tight to my neck-hair with your claws, while I swim across. As I must breathe hard, put the gem in your mouth. Mind that you don't open your jaws, or yawn, or laugh, till we get across. Do you hear?"

Mee Yow wagged her tail and took the wine-stone firmly in her mouth in token of determination to deliver that precious gem safely to her master. All the time Mee Yow intended to jump ashore and run to her master, while the dog would be shaking off the water from his hair, and thus get the credit for first finding where the stone had been.

It was a long, hard swim and the dog's strength was nearly used up when only two-thirds across the river, but the cat was happy, for she had only to hold on and keep her feet dry. All went well until near the opposite shore.

Now it happened just then that a party of children, out of school and ready for fun, caught sight of the odd pair. They had never seen anything so funny in all their lives, and at once they laughed uproariously. Snap was too serious to pay any attention to their glee, but Mee Yow, already tickled with vanity, became positively frivolous. She too joined with the children and laughed so hard that Snap's body was badly shaken, so that he nearly got his nose under water and drowned them both. This made the light-headed and conceited cat laugh all the more. Finally bursting in a guffaw, Mee Yow dropped the gem out of her mouth, so that it was hopelessly lost in the river and fell to the bottom.

That was too much for the dog, to have his labor thus wasted. Thinking only of his master the faithful and serious Snap dived to the bottom of the river, tumbling Mee Yow off. You may well believe though, much scratching and clawing took place before Puss let go and swam ashore.

Alas! the dog could not find the precious gem, and when once on land he first shook himself to dry his hair and then rushed at the cat to give her a good shaking. But Mee Yow climbed up a tree, and though nearly frozen to death after her icy bath, kept up growling as long as the dog barked.

After that, in Korea, the cats and dogs ceased to be friends. Indeed, they never spoke to each other. Wild, unloved and unpetted, the cat belongs to the bad animals in Tokgabi's museum, while the dog is the faithful friend of man.

CAT-KIN AND THE QUEEN MOTHER

Korea is called the Land of the Plum Blossom, but in winter the rivers freeze over. Then the men cut through the ice which is often several feet thick, to catch with their fishing lines and hooks the fish that swim in the water beneath. Yet they are very glad to welcome any sign of the coming spring, and they watch eagerly for the pussy willows to show themselves.

Now there was a farmer who lived in Nai-po, which is the grain garden of the Korean peninsula, who wanted a little daughter, though other parents cared more for sons.

One day farmer Pak, for that was his name, discovered a pussy willow which seemed to him, after the long winter, like a light shining in a dark place. He plucked it and carried proudly home this branch full of fuzzy little buds. This was a sign of his happiness at the return of spring. He was tired of ice and snow and now he knew that soon the gloomy hills would burst into a glory of bright colors from the blooming flowers, and look like an army with flags.

That same day his prayers were answered and a little girl was born into his home. Giving the pussy willow to his wife, he said: "We shall name our baby Cat-kin, that is Little Puss."

Cat-kin never saw a cradle, for the Korean mothers carry their babies on their backs. She was soon out of infancy, and then it was not long before she was standing up and toddling about and playing with her doggie and pet bull. These little pets on four legs usually take the place of kittens in a country home in Korea, for the cats are wild and do not allow children to fondle them.

Long before she was a dozen years old, Cat-kin became very fond of fairy stories, of which Korea has a great many, besides thousands of tales of wonderful people and animals and what happened to them. She often looked up towards the high hills and distant mountains, where she thought the fairies, dragons, ogres and tigers lived. Here also dwelt the sen-nin or mountain spirits, wise and good, of whom the old people talked and the soldiers painted on their banners when they went to war.

When about eight years old, Cat-kin wanted very much to walk up towards the north star, which her father showed her shining in the heavens. He had once traveled up into one of the Northern provinces, where during the daytime he could see afar off the great snow-white mass of the Ever White Mountain rising up to meet the azure sky. There, at the top he had heard, lay the Dragon Prince's Pool, out of which flowed the two rivers that made Korea an island. One was named the Tumen and the other the Yalu, after the beautiful green and blue sheen on the feathers of a drake's back, so richly colored were its shining waters. When her father told of his travels, Cat-kin also longed to go north to get to the very top and touch the sky.

But this she knew she could not do, even if she had had long legs and were as strong as a man, for the tigers were very numerous and always roaming about. These yellow and black striped brutes were man-eaters. They loved nothing better for a good dinner than a young girl.

So as she did not know any way of getting to the top of the Ever White Mountain and of seeing the deep blue waters of the Pool, except by riding on the back of a dragon, which she sometimes dreamed of, she kept waiting and waiting for one of these flying creatures to come, yet it never came.

Cat-kin was bound to have the fairies visit her, if possible. So one day, sitting under a persimmon tree and reading a story, she held the book in one hand, while she struck the ground several times, saying earnestly:

"Earth-spirit, earth-spirit, come to me; come up and see me."

All of a sudden the air seemed heavy with sweet perfume, and a silver mist like a cloud spread over her house and garden. Then a bright dazzling light flooded everything and there stood before her a glistening chariot, made of blue jade with golden wheels. It was drawn by milk-white horses and on a seat of shining silver sat the Western Heavenly Queen Mother herself.

Attendant upon the Mother Queen were thousands of the most beautiful maidens, who were all dressed in resplendent robes. They wore amber ornaments, and silver girdles, and necklaces of precious stones and silken robes with many tassels. Their feet were shod with gold embroidered velvet slippers, and on their heads were caps of gold studded with glittering gems. Cat-kin could hardly count the rich ornaments, necklaces, breast chains and the jade wands, like sceptres, which they held in their hands. These were shaped like lotus flowers. The faces of all these maidens were rosy, their eyes sparkled, and all had small hands and feet.

In a voice of great sweetness that sounded like music the Heavenly Queen Mother looked at Cat-kin and spoke to her, saying:

"Come forward, little maid, fear not. I shall take you with me to my palace, in the Island of Gems and give you all you want, besides showering blessings on your people, if you will come."

Cat-kin did not feel at all timid or frightened, but came boldly forward and knelt at the base of the chariot.

The Mother Queen first touched her with her milk-white jade wand, that was carved like a lotus bud, and made the little girl rise.

In a moment more, a silver chariot, with wheels made of turquoise and drawn by two young milk-white dragons, wheeled up close to her, and the attendant lady in golden robes bade her step in.

The dragons were fierce, powerful, fire-breathing creatures, with wide spreading wings, and their bodies and tails together were of the length of whales, while their eyes darted fire. Yet Cat-kin was not at all afraid, and thought it was great fun. Then up through and far above the clouds the host of bright beings flew. They followed the Queen Mother's chariot until, far away, they poised in mid-sky. Cat-kin was then told to look over the side of the chariot to the earth and ocean, miles and miles below. She was asked if she could recognize her father's cottage, but she could not. The whole village looked only like a grey mass of thatched roofs, and she could pick out only the temple.

There, spread out, was the great sea, as blue as a sapphire, and in places deep green, like an emerald, but she could see no ships nor any coast or shores, nor any ranges of mountains, nor signs of the land of Korea. Nothing but ripples and waves were visible. Yet in the center of the azure sea was an island. The trees were emeralds and the roofs of the houses were of gold, and the windows diamonds. These were so full of light that no lamps were necessary.

Beautiful beings, all maidens, as lovely in garb and face as those who filled the train of the Queen Mother, walked or played, or sang in the gardens. Or swam and sported in the sapphire waves, or rowed and sailed about in boats that seemed as if made of marble, they were so white.

At a signal from the Queen the singing ceased. Then there rose up wave upon wave of sweetest melody from the players on instruments who were in the gardens below.

Cat-kin thought she heard at intervals the chorus, sounding out the words, rising upward like pulses, through the air, "Welcome lovely mortal! Our Queen invites and we greet thee! Manifold be her gifts to thee and thine! Come, thou honored among all Korean maidens! Come to us and join our band and we shall love thee as one of ourselves."

In the wink of a falcon's eye- so short a time it seemed- the Mother Queen and her host descended.

As the chariots touched the island, a bevy of radiant maidens came forward, some to attend the Queen Mother and some to lead Cat-kin into her own room in the palace. There the most gorgeous robes were put on her, beside a cap begemmed with glittering, precious stones of various colors, and a pair of gold-embroidered velvet slippers.

Cat-kin was surprised when one of the shining maidens set a royal tiara adorned with five gems upon her brow.

"For me?" she asked in surprise.

"Yes for you, whom the Heavenly Mother Queen would honor."

"And what do these five gems, jade, crystal, malachite, amber and agate signify?" asked Cat-kin.

"Ah, that is not for us to tell you, but the Queen Mother ordered these. Tomorrow she will explain to you the secret of each gem."

Cat-kin walked about freely, enjoying the lovely sights and sounds. She also ate with keen appetite and to her full of the delicacies set on the table before her. Yet never once did she feel sleepy, nor see any beds, nor hear anyone talk of retiring. She wondered what they meant when they said "tomorrow"; for she could see no sun or moon or twilight. However, she did not think long about such things, and by and by forgot all about them.

When the entire court and all the hosts of the Queen Mother's attendants had assembled, Her Majesty's chamberlain read the proclamation, which declared that the Queen looked with great favor upon the Korean people, and had decided to bestow great gifts upon them. For this purpose, she had selected and brought to her palace the Korean maid named Cat-kin, to endow them through this, their daughter, with five precious traits of disposition and character. In token of gracious thought and tender love, Her Majesty would now present and explain the meaning of the five precious gems. These were jade, crystal, malachite, amber, and agate.

Cat-kin kneeled down before the Queen, who placed in Cat-kin's hands the shining gems, while an attendant fairy took them from her opened palm and placed each one of them on vermilion velvet, edged with gold. Then five maidens stood by, each with a gem laid on a cushion.

After the ceremony of presentation was over, the Queen made a speech, which told the Korean maiden's fortune and her future.

Cat-kin would be sent back over the clouds and ocean to the King's palace in the capital of her home land, and there be made a princess. Many nobles and king's sons from other countries, hearing of her beauty and her wonderful visit to the Island of Gems would come to pay her court as suitors. Many would ask for her hand, to be wedded to her; but she was to marry none but the king's son, a prince of her own people.

"Take these gems, fair maiden, and bestow their virtues and what they mean upon your people," said the Queen. "A thousand years from now- as men count time- we together will visit Korea again."

Then both the Queen and Cat-kin, stepping into the silver chariot, drawn by the fire-breathing dragons, plunged on and mounted up into space. First they sailed above the clouds and then dipped downwards, steering to Korea and over the mountains, bearing their precious charge to the capital. They reached the ground in a cloud and the wheels of the chariot stood still before the palace gate.

Yet before any mortal eyes could see their full forms, the Queen Mother and the dragons had disappeared, and Cat-kin stood alone, a resplendent maiden of dazzling appearance and in the robes given by the Heavenly Queen Mother, which all recognized at once as coming from the Island of Gems.

A throng of court ladies and palace attendants and a long line of nobles and princes were already waiting for the maiden, who they knew came gift-laden from the Queen Mother, of whom all had heard from childhood. The five gems were laid, each in a covered casket of perfumed wood, encrusted with gold on top and inlaid with mother-of-pearl.

Escorted into the throne room by a bevy of princesses, the Heavenly Mother's gifts in the five caskets were reverently placed on silken fans, spread out on a table having on its top the five cushions of crimson velvet.

Then, by lot and word of the diviners, the choice of a first drawing was awarded to a prince of fair face and mien. The other four nobles, one by one and in turn, approached and each was allowed to choose one of the caskets, all of which looked alike, and none was to be opened until the possessor was in his own home.

Now these were the gifts for body and mind, of which the polished gems were the tokens. According as each prince chose and received, so with the trait, which each gem signified, would his children and posterity be endowed. In the course of centuries, these would become the national features, of twenty millions of Koreans.

One by one the caskets were opened by each prince, and therein he discovered what was a trait in the character of the Korean people. These were:

Procrastination- Putting off until tomorrow, or some other time, what ought to be done today, and keeping back not only one person but the whole nation.

Hospitality- Always glad to see friends, to entertain people, even strangers, and to take care of relations, even to the making of one's self poor- a habit carried too far as the years and centuries rolled on.

Inexactness- The habit of not usually thinking clearly, counting correctly, or stating facts precisely, and when telling a story of "blowing a conch;" that is, of exaggerating.

Love of family- How the mothers and fathers in Korea do love their children, their kinsfolk and their relatives!

Sense of humor- A Korean can always see the funny side of things. He loves to joke and he bears his troubles well, because he likes to smile. As for the girls, they laugh as easily as the rain falls, or the flowers bloom.

And what the Queen Mother predicted came true. Just as five fingers make up the hand, so the average people among the Koreans are known by the five traits, for better or for worse.

THE MAGIC PEACH

Out on the ocean, so far away that no ship ever sailed there, is an island on which stood the seven storied palace of the royal lady, Su Wang Moo. In our language, this title means Western Queen Mother. She is always ready to help good mortals with her gifts and favors.

On this island thousands of genii wait to obey the commands of the Queen Mother. She has also chariots of silver and gold drawn by dragons, by which she sends her messages everywhere.

The genii and most of the shining maidens stay at home to fulfill the Queen's commands. In addition to these servants, she has hundreds of azure pigeons, which she often despatches to far-off places. In their bills, or under their wings, they carry some gift or promise to make people happy.

In the mind of many a Korean maiden there rises the dream, or there wells up the hope, that some day the Western Queen Mother will send to her pretty clothes of silk, with necklaces of jewels, a handsome youth to wed her, and a silver ring for the marriage ceremony.

Then she pictures to herself how splendidly she will be arrayed and how fine she will look in the costume of a bride; how her long black hair will be done up very high, with flowers and rosettes over the crown of her head, and ermine-edged slippers will be put on her feet. She wonders how she will feel when she drinks the cups of sacramental wine that make her a wife, after which she will go with her husband and bow to the memorial tablets of his ancestors.

She goes all over in her mind the happy times she will have in her husband's home. What she hopes for most, after all these things, is to have a kind mother-in-law. Then she will be a queen in her own little kingdom, with plenty of rice and kimchi, and cakes and goodies.

So it is that many Korean maidens go out under the blue sky to look up at the stars, or on moonlight nights scan the heavens to see if the birds are coming. Hoping to greet the azure pigeons, they put on their best clothes and watch. Many are their dreams.

Oh! how many lads also dream of the genii and of the riding on the dragon's back, to cross the mountain ranges and the great oceans, and to visit strange, far-off countries; or, they think of the pink coat which they will wear. The pink coat shows that the lad is engaged to be married and will, when grown up, be a husband to the little girl who may be in her cradle days; for in Korea children and even babies in arms are engaged to be married to other children.

Then the boy pictures the day when the long braid of hair, which he now has to wear down his back, shall be tucked up into a topknot, like a man's. No matter how old a bachelor may be, he must wear this boy's braid of hair. He must not speak, or talk with his elders, without first asking permission. He must be "seen and not heard" in company, and every one treats him as a child. So the boy also waits for the azure pigeons to come, for to be engaged to be married even when quite young, or to have a wife when older, means a great deal.

Then the young husband will wear a wide brimmed hat after school and go up to the city, with his fellow villagers, to try at the literary examinations. They will all march together, under a banner tufted at the top with pheasant feathers. If he passes successfully, he will be welcomed home with a parade and band of music. By and by, he will become a magistrate and have a string of amber beads over his ear, and wear on his breast a square of gold-embroidered velvet. Servants will carry him in a palanquin and his men will carry wooden paddles to punish folks who break the laws. Then he can strut about, in starched white flowing clothes, with the common people all afraid of him. No wonder that the boy waits for the coming of the blue pigeon!

Now in the gardens of the Queen's Palace, on the Island of Gems, there grow wonderful fruits of a rich, ripe color, brilliant with light and sheen. These, when served at the banquets and eaten, have the power of making the guest live very long, even for thousands of years.

Especially powerful is the celestial peach of longevity, which is served on little golden tables, its juice makes an old person's body new, so that one who eats the peach will live hundreds of years.

Sometimes the Queen sends one of these fruits to her favorites on the earth. Yet no one can ever get any of these peaches, unless the Queen herself gives them, and the peach trees are always jealously guarded by genii and dragons. None, even of the Queen's servants, or her waiting maids, or any of the genii, or dragons, can bestow the peach of longevity on mortals.

Now it happened that the Queen, hearing of the virtues of a certain king's son, despatched one of her lovely maidens, in one of her ten thousand dragon chariots, inviting him to visit Her Majesty, in the Island of Gems. She sent a message also to the prince's parents, telling them that their son would return before the end of the moon, which was then in its first quarter.

His anxious mother, who had a bride already picked out for her son to wed, warned him against looking too long at the lovely princesses, or pretty maids in the Queen's Palace of Gems. In truth she had her lurking suspicions. She feared for her darling son, that, beneath their rosy faces and moon-like eyes, they were really sirens, possibly even sea monsters in female form, and might eat him up.

She also urged him to be very careful as to etiquette. He must be especially decorous, because the code of behavior and manners might not be the same as those among polite people upon the earth. Moreover, he must notice and hear everything and, when he came back home, tell her all about it.

On the other hand, the Queen of the Island of Gems warned the lovely maiden, a princess whom she sent, to beware lest the prince might fall in love with her, either on the way, or when at the island. If he tried to persuade her to marry him and to stay on the earth and not come back to the Island of Gems, and to her duties to the Queen, the palace maid would be disgraced and die early.

Although the Queen laughed when she said it, and quoted the proverb, "Don't trust a pigeon to carry grain," she was really very serious, and the maiden knew that it would not do to thwart the royal wishes.

So this discreet princess made a firm resolve to be very careful. She decided that when she met the prince she would be very cold in her bearing. When delivering the Queen's invitation, she would appear to think it only a matter of business, though very important. She would not stay more than an hour in the prince's mansion.

When the dragon chariot was returning homeward she would be silent. She would hold no conversation, nor speak a word, nor let the prince sit beside her, but she would keep in the front seat nearest the dragon, while he should ride on the great creature's back.

So it was a very quiet journey which the prince made, while the chariot sped over the clouds, with the earth and oceans lying far beneath. Part of the time he sat on the dragon's back, as if in a saddle, but after a while he climbed back into the chariot again, and all the time he was so thrilled with the speed and the grandeur of it all that, to tell the truth, he forgot all about the lovely princess who had brought the Queen's message, until he found himself at the Queen's Palace of Gems and was invited to step out of the chariot.

Soon he was seated with others, similarly honored, at the table which was loaded down with dishes of gold and silver which were heaped with the choicest viands. The guests, all in fine clothes like the prince, were waited on by shining maidens of exquisite beauty and robed in golden garments gemmed with glittering jewels of the most precious workmanship.

Upon one of these lovely creatures, a maiden who seemed to be about sixteen, not far away from where he sat, the prince cast his eyes. She was kneeling on the floor ready to do his bidding. He was so filled with admiration at her loveliness that he could hardly pay any attention to the talk at the table. Despite his mother's warning, he made several mistakes in propriety.

Yet his appetite was very good after his long journey and he ate heartily of the delicious fare. Towards the end of the feast, feeling in a jolly mood, he picked up one of the peaches. Then he pared and sliced it, greatly enjoying its juicy nectar. Every morsel of the pulp, as he put it in his mouth, made him feel as if he were gaining a century of vigor. He knew he was lengthening his life and increasing his power to enjoy the pleasures of which he had always been very fond.

Indeed the prince was far less of a scholar and student than he ought to have been. Often at home when his teachers were all present and ready to begin the tasks of the day, the lad was still out at play. His older sister used to say laughingly of her brother, "He never let his studies interfere with his education."

Yet every moment this maiden kneeling near him seemed to grow more charming in both face and form, dress and adornment, ease and grace of motion. Indeed she seemed the very embodiment of all loveliness, and the prince could not keep his eyes off her. He did not know that this was the effect of eating the peach of longevity, for the maiden was really no prettier at the end of the banquet than she had been at the beginning. The change was in him, not in her.

So intoxicated was the prince, that he so far forgot himself and what his mother had told him not to do, that he picked out one of the finest-looking of the peaches from its golden basket on the table and tossed it over to the pretty maiden.

On her part the maid of honor had herself been so wrapped up in admiration of the young and princely guest, that when he motioned that he was about to toss a peach to her she broke the rule of the Palace of Gems. She threw out her hands and caught the peach deftly, as if playing ball.

The palace ladies were all horrified. They had been taught that, except to perform the duties of waiting and serving, they were to pay no attention to anything the guests might say or do. When heated with wine the guests might be only making sport of the attendants. They were to decline any personal attentions and continue in their duty of serving. But instead of averting her gaze, or bowing low with her face to the ground, or having her eyes downcast, the maid, actually threw out her hands, caught the peach and, to the horror of all who saw her, bit into it and swallowed the morsel.

What it was that happened the very next moment even the fairies could not tell or exactly remember; for a golden mist seemed to fall in the banquet hall, enveloping everything.

It happens that just here in the story a great gap occurs. At such a pause the Korean story-teller, who sits in his booth in one of the back streets of Seoul, would stop and send his boy to take up a collection from the crowd. Nor would he go on, until all had been invited to give and the coins rattled in the gourd shell.

When he began again some said it was the same story continued. Others were sure it was a new story, but that the palace maid and the prince were the same who had been in the banquet hall of the Western Queen Mother, in the Island of Gems and that the peach had never lost, since it never could lose its virtues, because given by the Queen. But such as it was, this is the way the story ran on:

-More than a thousand years afterwards it was known that in the high mountains of the Ever White range lived a holy man, a hermit, who was honored, almost worshiped by the people in that region. In the summer time hundreds of pilgrims visited his hut to hear wise words about how to live and do good, and then to receive the hermit's blessing. Even the wild beasts appeared to be tame in his presence. At any rate, they never tried to bite or devour one another, or hurt the old man or to destroy his humble shelter. The tigers, the leopards and the bears seemed to forget they had claws, or teeth; while their little cubs played peacefully with each other.

The dress of this hermit was of the ancient style of a thousand years before, of the time of the ancient dynasty of Ko.

One day while out on one of his walks this old, white-bearded hermit met a woman of fair countenance, who seemed to be quite young, for her face was unwrinkled and rosy. It appeared that she had travelled far, yet she walked with the springing step of a maiden who was still in her teens. Her dress betokened that of ages gone, for it was of the sort and fashion which are revealed in the cave pictures painted on the walls of the dolmens, or the colossal stone chambers, in which kings and mighty men were buried, ten or fifteen centuries ago, which are very many in Korea.

The hermit and maid met in the path under the tall pine tree and exchanged greetings, the lady bowing very low. Then, as she looked up in his eyes, her face became radiant with joy as if she recognized a dear friend.

The sage inquired who she was, and whether she were the wandering lady, of whom rumor spoke of having been seen during centuries, over all the nine provinces of Korea, by people who were great grandfathers, as well as by the children of that day.

Then she told her story.

-She was the same palace maid, who, in the Western Queen Mother's palace on the Island of Gems had waited upon him, once a gay prince and now the holy hermit. Then again she bowed low.

For catching and eating the peach which the princely guest had tossed to her, and thus breaking the rules of the palace, the Queen had ordered her banishment for a thousand years.

But during all this time she had been seeking the prince who tossed her the peach of longevity; for she knew that neither she nor he could die, till the thousand years had passed. Yet none of the men she met, however handsome, learned or wealthy, reached her ideal of the youth she had seen so long ago. Not finding him, she went back to the Island of Gems, traveling on a dragon's back, and humbly begged the Queen to extend her term of life, until she should meet the one she loved so dearly, even if she found him only after hundreds of years more of wandering and of hope deferred.

The Mother Queen listened to her petition and was gracious and extended the maiden's life. So on the earth she kept up her wanderings. Now, having met the holy hermit she was happy, for she felt sure that she had found the same prince, venerable in appearance though he was, for she could see his soul.

The hermit listened with delight to the lady's story of her life in the palace and of her wanderings, during a thousand years in search of one she loved; and, especially, that she had been willing to have the Mother Queen order her future.

As for the hermit, his long white beard which swept his breast fell off, his bald head was in a moment covered with luxuriant black hair, and he became young again in her presence, with springing step and bright eyes. He could not be more rosy in countenance, for the pure life he had led had kept his skin pink. They spent many hours together, in talking long and joyfully over their experiences in the Island of Gems.

Then both agreed that now, since they had met again, they would bow gladly to the Queen's decision concerning them both, and do whatever Her Majesty ordered.

But already by a flying dragon that was famous for gathering up news from all parts of the universe, the Queen had been told of the meeting of the lovers in the mountain path, and of their pious resolve to commit their future to Her Majesty in the Island of Gems.

Suddenly the pair of lovers heard near the mountain top a sound of sweet music, as of some fairy playing on a lute, and at every second the sounds seemed to come lower and nearer. Soon a great white cloud of sweet smelling odors, like incense, enveloped them. What was their surprise to see a golden chariot drawn by two dragons, whose eyes were like emeralds, come up close to where they stood. Both of them, prince-hermit and maid were then taken up into the chariot and borne swiftly over cloud, and mountain and sea, to the Island of Gems. There the Queen ordered them to be married, and, after a splendid wedding, they lived happily ever after.

THE GREAT STONE FIRE EATER

Ages ago, there lived a great Fire Spirit inside of a mountain to the southwest of Seoul, the capital of Korea. He was always hungry and his food was anything that would burn. He devoured trees, forests, dry grass, wood, and whatever he could get hold of. When those were not within his reach, he ate stones and rocks. He enjoyed the flames, but threw the hard stuff out of his mouth in the form of lava.

This Fire Monster spent most of his time in a huge volcano some distance away, but in sight of the capital. The city people used to watch the smoke coming out of the crater by day and issuing in red fire, between sunset and sunrise, until all the heavens seemed in flames. Then, they said, the Fire Spirit was lighting up his palace. On cloudy nights the inside of the volcano glowed like a furnace. The moulten mass inside the crater was reflected on the clouds, so that one could almost see into the monster's belly.

But nothing tasted so good to the Fire Eater as things which men built, such as houses, stables, fences, and general property. An especial titbit, that he longed to swallow, was the royal palace.

Looking out of its crater one day, he saw the king's palace all silver bright and brand new, rising in the City of Seoul. Thereupon he chuckled, and said to himself, for he was very happy:

"There's a feast for me! I'll just walk out of my mountain home and eat up that dainty morsel. I wonder how the king will like it."

But the Fire Spirit was in no hurry. He felt sure of his meal. So he waited until his friend, the South Wind, was prepared to join him.

"Let me know when you're ready," said the Fire Spirit to the South Wind, "and we'll have a splendid blaze. We'll go up at night and enjoy a lively dance before they can get a drop of water on us. Don't let the rain-clouds know anything about our picnic."

The South Wind promised easily, for she was always glad to have a frolic.

So when the sun went down and it was dark, the Fire Spirit climbed out of his rocky home in the volcano and strode toward Seoul. The South Wind pranced and capered with him until the streets of the capital were so gusty that no one with a wide-brimmed hat dared go outdoors, lest, in a lively puff, he might lose his head-gear. As for the men in mourning, who wear straw hats a yardstick wide and as big and deep as wash-tubs, they locked themselves up at home and played checkers. By the time all the palace guards were asleep the Fire Spirit was ready. He said to the South Wind:

"Blow, blow, your biggest blast, as I begin to touch the roofs of the smaller houses. This will whet my appetite for the palace, and then together we'll eat them all up."

Not till they heard a mighty roar and crackling did the people in Seoul push back their paper windows to find out what was the matter. Oh, what a blaze! It seemed to mount to heaven with red tongues that licked the stars. Those who could see in the direction of the palace supposed the sun had risen, but soon the crash of falling roofs and mighty columns of smoke and flame, with clouds of sparks, told the terrible story. By the time the sun did rise, there was nothing but a level waste of ashes, where the large buildings had been. Even the smoke had been driven away by the wind.

When the king and his people in the palace enclosure, who had saved their lives by running fast, thought over their loss, they began to plan how to stop the Fire Monster, when he should take it into his head to saunter forth on another walk and gobble up the king's dwelling.

A council of wise men was called to decide upon the question. Many long heads were bowed in hard thought over the matter. All the firemen, stone-cutters, fortune-tellers, dragon tamers, geomancers and people skilled in preventing conflagrations were invited to give their advice about the best way to fight the hungry Fire Demon.

After weeks spent in pondering the problem they all agreed that a dragon from China should be brought over to Korea. If kept in a swamp and fed well, he would surely prevent the Fire Imp from rambling too near Seoul. Besides, the dragon knew how to amuse and persuade the South Wind not to join in the mischief.

So, at tremendous cost and trouble, one of China's biggest dragons, capable of making rain and of spouting tons of water on its enemies, was shipped over and kept in a swamp. It was honored with a royal decoration, allowed to wear a string of amber beads over its ear, given a horsehair hat, a nobleman's girdle and fed all the turnips it desired to eat. In every way it was treated as the king's favorite.

But it was all in vain. Money and favor were alike wasted. The petted dragon made it rain too often, so that the land was soaked. Then when told not to do this, it grew sulky and neglected its duty. Finally it became fat and lazy and one night fell asleep when it ought to have been on guard, for the winds were out on a dance.

Seeing his jailer thus caught napping, the Fire Imp leaped out of its volcano prison, rode quickly on the South Wind to Seoul and in a few hours had again swallowed the royal palace. There was nothing seen next day except ashes, which the Fire Monster cared no more for than we for nutshells when the kernels are eaten up.

With big tears in their eyes, the king and his wise men met together again to decide on a new scheme to keep off the Fire Imp. They were ready to drown him, or to see him get eaten up, because he had twice swallowed up the palace. They sent the Chinese dragon home and this time, besides the fortune-tellers and the stone-cutters, the well-diggers were invited also. For many days the wise men studied maps, talked of geography, looked at mountains, valleys, and the volcano, and studied air currents. Finally one man, famous for his deep learning about wood and water, forests and rivers, spoke thus:

"It is evident that the fire has always come from the southwest and up this valley," pointing to a map.

"True, true," shouted all the wise men.

"Well, right in his path let us dig a big pond, a regular artificial lake and very deep, into which the Fire Monster will tumble. This will put him out and he can get no further."

"Agreed, agreed," shouted the wise men in chorus. "Why did we not think of this before?"

All the skilful diggers of wells and ditches were summoned to the capital. With shovel and spade they worked for weeks. Then they let in water from the river until the pond was full.

So everybody in Seoul went to bed thinking that the king's palace was now safe surely.

But the Fire Imp, seeing the dragon gone and his opportunity come, climbed out of his volcano and moved out for another meal. This time, the South Wind was busy elsewhere and could not go with him. So he went alone, but coming to the pond, tumbled and wet himself so badly that he was chilled and nearly put out when he got to the palace, which was only half burned. So he went home growling and hungry.

Again the wise men were called and the first thing they did was to thank the boss well-digger, who had made the pond. The king summoned him into his presence to confer rank upon him and his children. He was presented with four rolls of silk, forty pounds of white ginseng, a tiger-skin robe, sixty dried chestnuts and forty-four strings of copper cash. Loaded with such Korean wealth and honors, the man fell on his hands and knees and thanked His Majesty profusely.

Then they called the master stone-cutter or chief of the guild and asked him if he could chisel out the figure of a beast that could eat flames and be ugly enough to scare away the Fire Imp.

The master had long hoped that he would be invited to rear this bit of sculpture, but hitherto the king and Court had feared it might cost too much.

So the order was given, and out of the heart of the mountains, a mighty block of white granite was loosed and brought to Seoul on rollers, pushed, pulled, and hoisted by thousands of laborers. Then, hidden behind canvas, to keep the matter secret, lest the Fire Imp should find it out, the workmen toiled. Hammers and chisels clinked, until on a certain day the Great Stone Flame Eater was ready to take his permanent seat in front of the palace gate, as guardian of the royal buildings and treasures.

The Fire Imp laughed when the South Wind told him of what the Koreans in the capital were doing, even though she warned him of the danger of his being eaten up.

"I shall walk out and see for myself anyhow," said the Fire Imp.

One night he crept out quietly and moved toward the city. He was nearly drowned in the pond, but plucking up courage, he went on until he was near the king's dwelling. Hearing the Fire Imp coming, the Great Flame Eater turned his head and licked his chops in anticipation of swallowing the Fire Imp whole, as a toad does a fly.

But one sight of the hideous stony monster was enough for the Fire Imp. There, before him, on a high pedestal was something never before seen in heaven or on earth. It had enormous fire-proof scales like a salamander, with curly hair like asbestos and its mouth was full of big fangs. It was altogether hideous enough to give even a Volcano Spirit a chill.

"Just think of those jaws snapping on me," said the Fire Imp to himself, as he looked at them and the fangs. "I do believe that creature is half alligator and half water-tortoise. I had better go home. No dinner this time!"

So by his freezing glance alone, the Great Flame Eater frightened away the Fire Imp, so that he never came again and the royal palace was not once burned. To-day the ugly brute still keeps watch. You have only to look at him to enjoy this story.

PIGLING AND HER PROUD SISTER

Pear Blossom had been the name of a little Korean maid who was suddenly left motherless. When her father, Kang Wa, who was a magistrate high in office, married again, he took for his wife a proud widow whose daughter, born to Kang Wa, was named Violet. Mother and daughter hated housework and made Pear Blossom clean the rice, cook the food and attend to the fire in the kitchen. They were hateful in their treatment of Pear Blossom, and, besides never speaking a kind word, called her Pigling, or Little Pig, which made the girl weep often.

It did no good to complain to her father, for he was always busy. He smoked his yard-long pipe and played checkers hour by hour, apparently caring more about having his great white coat properly starched and lustred than for his daughter to be happy. His linen had to be beaten with a laundry club until it glistened like hoar frost, and, except his wide-brimmed black horsehair hat, he looked immaculately white when he went out of the house to the Government office.

Poor Pigling had to perform this task of washing, starching and glossing, in addition to the kitchen work and the rat-tat-tat of her laundry stick was often heard in the outer room till after midnight, when her heartless stepsister and mother had long been asleep.

There was to be a great festival in the city and for many days preparations were made in the house to get the father ready in his best robe and hat, and the women in their finery, to go out and see the king and the royal procession.

Poor Pigling wanted very much to have a look at the pageant, but the cruel stepmother, setting before her a huge straw bag of unhulled rice and a big cracked water jar, told her she must husk all the rice, and, drawing water from the well, fill the crock to the brim before she dared to go out on the street.

What a task to hull with her fingers three bushels of rice and fill up a leaky vessel! Pigling wept bitterly. How could it ever be done?

While she was brooding thus and opening the straw bag to begin spreading the rice out on mats, she heard a whir and a rush of wings and down came a flock of pigeons. They first lighted on her head and shoulders, and then hopping to the floor began diligently, with beak and claw, and in a few minutes the rice lay in a heap, clean, white, and glistening, while with their pink toes they pulled away the hulls and put these in a separate pile.

Then, after a great chattering and cooing, the flock was off and away.

Pigling was so amazed at this wonderful work of the birds that she scarcely knew how to be thankful enough. But, alas, there was still the cracked crock to be filled. Just as she took hold of the bucket to begin there crawled out of the fire hole a sooty black imp, named Tokgabi.

"Don't cry," he squeaked out. "I'll mend the broken part and fill the big jar for you." Forthwith, he stopped up the crack with clay, and pouring a dozen buckets of water from the well into the crock, it was filled to brimming and the water spilled over on all sides. Then Tokgabi the imp bowed and crawled into the flues again, before the astonished girl could thank her helper.

So Pigling had time to dress in her plain but clean clothes that were snow-white. She went off and saw the royal banners and the king's grand procession of thousands of loyal men.

The next time, the stepmother and her favorite daughter planned a picnic on the mountain. So the refreshments were prepared and Pigling had to work hard in starching the dresses to be worn- jackets, long skirts, belts, sashes, and what not, until she nearly dropped with fatigue. Yet instead of thanking and cheering her, the cruel stepmother told Pigling she must not go out until she had hoed all the weeds out of the garden and pulled up all the grass between the stones of the walk.

Again the poor girl's face was wet with tears. She was left at home alone, while the others went off in fine clothes, with plenty to eat and drink, for a day of merrymaking.

While weeping thus, a huge black cow came along and out of its great liquid eyes seemed to beam compassion upon the kitchen slave. Then, in ten mouthfuls, the animal ate up the weeds, and, between its hoof and lips, soon made an end of the grass in the stone pathway.

With her tears dried Pigling followed this wonderful brute out over the meadows into the woods, where she found the most delicious fruit her eyes ever rested upon. She tasted and enjoyed, feasting to the full and then returned home.

When the jealous stepsister heard of the astonishing doings of the black cow, she determined to enjoy a feast in the forest also. So on the next gala-day she stayed home and let the kitchen drudge go to see the royal parade. Pigling could not understand why she was excused, even for a few hours, from the pots and kettles, but she was still more surprised by the gift from her stepmother of a rope of cash to spend for dainties. Gratefully thanking the woman, she put on her best clothes and was soon on the main street of the city enjoying the gay sights and looking at the happy people. There were tight rope dancing, music with drum and flute by bands of strolling players, tricks by conjurers and mountebanks, with mimicking and castanets, posturing by the singing girls and fun of all sorts. Boys peddling honey candy, barley sugar and sweetmeats were out by the dozen. At the eating-house, Pigling had a good dinner of fried fish, boiled rice with red peppers, turnips, dried persimmons, roasted chestnuts and candied orange, and felt as happy as a queen.

The selfish stepsister had stayed home, not to relieve Pigling of work, but to see the wonderful cow. So, when the black animal appeared and found its friend gone and with nothing to do, it went off into the forest.

The stepsister at once followed in the tracks of the cow but the animal took it into its head to go very fast, and into unpleasant places. Soon the girl found herself in a swamp, wet, miry and full of brambles. Still hoping for wonderful fruit, she kept on until she was tired out and the cow was no longer to be seen. Then, muddy and bedraggled, she tried to go back, but the thorny bushes tore her clothes, spoiled her hands and so scratched her face that when at last, nearly dead, she got home, she was in rags and her beauty was gone.

But Pigling, rosy and round, looked so lovely that a young man from the south, of good family and at that time visiting the capital, was struck with her beauty. And as he wanted a wife, he immediately sought to find out where she lived. Then he secured a go-between who visited both families and made all the arrangements for the betrothal and marriage.

Grand was the wedding. The groom, Su-wen, was dressed in white and black silk robes, with a rich horsehair cap and head-dress denoting his rank as a Yang-ban, or gentleman. On his breast, crossed by a silver-studded girdle, was a golden square embroidered with flying cranes rising above the waves- the symbols of civil office. He was tall, handsome, richly cultured, and quite famous as a writer of verses, besides being well read in the classics.

Charming, indeed, looked Pear Blossom as she was now called again, in her robe of brocade, and long undersleeves which extended from her inner dress of snow-white silk. Dainty were her red kid shoes curved upward at the toes. With a baldric of open-worked silver, a high-waisted long skirt, with several linings of her inner silk robes showing prettily at the neck, and the silver bridal ring on her finger, she looked as lovely as a princess.

Besides her bridal dower, her father asked Pear Blossom what she preferred as a special present. When she told him, he laughed heartily. Nevertheless he fulfilled her wishes and to this day, in the boudoir of Pear Blossom, now Mrs. Su-wen, there stands an earthen figure of a black cow moulded and baked from the clay of her home province, while the pigeons like to hover about a pear tree that bursts into bloom every spring time and sheds on the ground a snowy shower of fragrant petals.

THE MIRROR THAT MADE TROUBLE

The city of Seoul lies near the Han river, which flows all the way across Korea from the high mountains to the level sea. To most Korean people, in the old days when no one traveled abroad, Seoul was the center of the universe.

All roads in the kingdom led to this wonderful city, in which there were big shops and stores, and gay streets full of lively people in rich clothing. The gentlemen in their stiffly starched and glistening white clothes walked very proudly with their heads up in the air. When they straddled the little Korean ponies, which are not much bigger than Newfoundland dogs, it seemed as if elephants were trying to ride on donkeys.

From morning to night the avenues were full of traffic and business. All the wonderful things brought by the Arabs from India, and by the merchants from Japan and China, could be bought in the Korean capital.

A thousand bulls loaded with dry grass and fire-wood came through the city gates into Seoul every day. They could be seen passing along, but not much besides legs, tail and horns were visible. At breakfast and supper time clouds of blue smoke rose up from ten thousand low, and often underground chimneys, carrying the heat and fire from the kitchens, where good things to eat were cooked. The cartloads of bags of rice, millet, barley, fruits and vegetables, goodies and cookies, jars and crockery, seen in the shops, would make a mountain.

Palaces, pagodas, temples and mansions of the nobles and wealthy people made the place in which the king lived very beautiful, while out beyond were the high stone city walls, white or covered with vines.

When the sun dipped below the mountains the gates were shut, and after that no one could enter until morning. At every closing and opening of the gates the musicians played lively tunes and the great bell tolled out the time of sunrise and sunset. In the band were drums, fifes, trumpets and stringed instruments.

At night from inside the house and wineshops, one could hear the sounds of revelry, music, song, dancing and feasting, which often lasted till morning.

Out on the Great South Mountain, a mighty fire burned and the flames shot high up in the air. This was the welcome message that all was peaceful throughout the whole kingdom. On hilltop and mountain, from the snowy peaks of the Ever White Mountain to the islands out in the Southern Sea, and from the east to the west coast, these signal fires blaze. Flame answering flame made a telegraph announcing that all was well.

But at nine o'clock Seoul outdoors was a woman's city. All boys and men must be off the streets. Any male person caught by the police would be taken to the magistrate's office and there receive a severe beating with wooden paddles by the public spankers. Then the women and grown-up girls, old and young, went outdoors, breathed the air, took their walks, made their visits, and had a delightful time with play and chat and gossip. But by midnight every one must be indoors.

It was no wonder then that in the country the farmers and the village folk thought that Seoul, the capital, was the most splendid city on earth. If they ever heard of London and Paris and New York, they supposed that these places on the map were only villages. How was it possible that any city could equal or surpass Seoul? Why, the very idea was nonsense!

In every hamlet even the children hoped some day to see the city. Often they dreamed of riding through the air on a dragon's back in order to get there. It was thought that anything which a mortal man or even the insatiable Tokgabi should require, could be bought in Seoul.

Now in a village up north, which in English we should call Cucumberville, lived a miller, Mr. Kim and his wife Cho. The man had worked hard for many years and heaped up piles of iron and brass cash, which he kept hidden under a rafter beneath the roof. He had long intended to see the royal city, and his wife encouraged him, for she wanted a new dress, and a comb and a pair of shoes, such as city people wear. His daughters said they would like to have girdles, ermine-trimmed slippers and silver hair pins. Kim felt that he must surely go, to please both himself and his family.

So one fine May morning he started off to walk to Seoul and see the sights. His wife and daughters, bowing down with their faces to the paper carpet, begged him to bring them the pretty things they talked about so much, and also whatever might please himself.

His faithful spouse bade him beware of thieves and robbers and not to let his money lie around loose in the inns by the way. When in Seoul he must not go into the wineshops, or to see the dancing girls called ge-sang (or geisha), or to spend his cash foolishly. There were many wicked men about and she had heard that beside the polite people there were boors even in the capital. This she thought must surely be the fact, for there was a proverb that said so.

On his part Kim cautioned his wife, since it was still chilly weather, to keep the kitchen fires burning, so as to have the house warm and not let the girls take cold. She must beware also of robbers. These bad men had the habit of coming after midnight, when the fire was out, and of quietly loosening the stones of the foundations under the floor and getting inside, and also into the rooms through the flues. The house must be well locked up and the door barricaded at night, so that no prowling leopard or tiger roaming around should get in. If she heard any scratching or clawing on the roof, she was to strike the gong. This would alarm the villagers, and then the men would rush out with torches and drive off the beasts of prey. If she should hear the pigs squealing out in the pen, she must sound the alarm for the tigers loved Korean pork even more than Korean people.

Now Kim was a first-rate fellow. When at home he was pretty sharp at a bargain while buying beans, millet or rice, and was skilful in grinding barley or chopping up straw for the donkeys. But when he was once inside the walls of the big city, one would think "he carried his head under his armpits," as the Koreans say.

For amid so many strange sights and sounds he was dazed. Like a great gawk he stood on the main street, with his mouth open. As the crowds went by, he wondered where all the people came from, and how they all got a living.

He found the saying true that "There are rude people, even in Seoul," for one fellow shouted at him asking him whether he intended to swallow the moon. Some of the boys laughed at him and one said his mouth was like a bird box, and something might fly in.

Kim looked at many things in the shops, but when he asked how much they cost he nearly fainted. He was truly scared at the price, and walked on. However, he bought some pretty things for his wife and daughters, such as a fan, a roll of silk for a dress, a box of hairpins, some amber beads, and a silver ring, so that when his oldest daughter, who was soon to marry, became a bride, she would have everything ready.

While in the silk shop the clerk who sold him the goods saw that Kim was from the country and thought he would have a little fun. So he told Kim about the fairies, and pointed out a shop across the way. There, if he looked at the round thing which the shop man would gladly show him, he would see and feel as he never felt or saw before.

At once Kim went across the street and over to the shop, where they made metal things, bright, shining, polished and silvery. There he stood in front of a round thing like the moon. In it was a man's face. It was the face of some one he thought he knew. It was a man about his own age he fancied, yet he could not tell just who it was or call him by name, but he was sure he had seen the person before. When he turned around suddenly, hoping to surprise a friend, and perhaps a neighbor, from his home town, there was nobody near. He looked again. There it was! Had his friend hid himself and then come back?

When Kim dodged he lost sight of the face, but when standing in front of this round thing, there was the same man again in the mirror, for that is what the shining metal was.

When Kim laughed the fellow laughed too. When he made a wry face or grimaces, the other person, whoever he was, did the same. No matter how quickly Kim might turn around to catch him, he was gone.

Now Kim had never before seen a mirror and did not know

what it might be. Yet thinking it was almost like fairy magic, he bought the metal disc and took it back with him.

When he arrived home he must first of all unpack the boxes containing the pretty things for the women of his family, for the girls were impatient to see what their father had brought them.

They were so absorbed in their gifts that they did not notice what Mr. Kim had bought for himself. So he laid the case containing the mirror on the table and put some other purchases away in the big cabinet, inlaid with mother-of-pearl, that stood in the best room. Then he went out to look after his mill, and the pigs, the donkey, and the bull.

No sooner had the girls opened the mirror case, than terrible things happened. The mother, who was behind the daughter, saw the face of a young woman and was startled at beholding a stranger, as she thought, in her house. Instantly she broke out in a fit of jealous passion.

"Your father has brought home another woman, a ge-sang, from Seoul, to take my place. What does he mean?"

At the same time the daughter, seeing a face in the polished metal, cried out, "No mother, we won't have any strange woman in your place. Besides she's too young and will be a tyrant to us."

Hearing the loud voices and crying, the grandmother hobbled in and asked what was the matter.

"Look, see for yourself, what our daddy has brought home to us to make us miserable."

Seeing the mirror, Granny looked into it for a moment. Then she too burst into a passion, and cried out, "I won't have this old woman in our house. It's enough for my son to support me and his family. Oh, why did he go to Seoul?"

By this time there was such a racket with four women, young, middle-aged, and old, crying so lustily, that each one quickly used up three paper handkerchiefs apiece, before they could dry their tears.

While still crying out, "ugo, ugo!" very loudly, grandfather came in, shaking his stick and ordering them to be quiet. Then, looking at their streaming faces and dropping tears, he demanded to know the cause of the trouble.

"See for yourself," said his wife. Then she handed him the metal trouble-maker, such as had never before been seen in the village.

At once the old man turned almost purple with rage.

"What," cried he in his cracked voice, "is my son so unfilial as to bring another old man into the house? How can he support two fathers? Where will he get the kimchi and millet for the old fellow to eat?" Then he threw the mirror into its box and slammed down the lid tight.

All this time while jealousy was eating up these angry people and threatening to disrupt the family, the noise increased so greatly, that the husband left his pigs and his mill, and rushed in to see what was the matter.

At once his wife, who was a very strong woman, flew at him, and seizing his topknot, pulled him and dragged him over the floor and outdoors, and along into the street, never stopping till she reached the house of the judge to tell her troubles. There she made out a terrible story.

Once in the presence of the great man who wore a mighty hat and had a string of amber beads hung over his ear, she told the story of what her husband had brought from Seoul, to destroy the peace of his family. Surely, he meant to go back to the capital and have a young wife! In her anger her tongue never stopped a moment.

She charged her husband with all the crimes known in the codes. Yet all that she could prove against him was that he had brought something round, made of metal, into the house. She assured the judge that it was as full of evil magic as Tokgabi and all his imps.

Now the other members of the family joined in accusation of the miller. Besides supporting the wife's story, they all declared that it was true in every detail; because the five witnesses all agreed in their story.

When the flood of talk had subsided somewhat, the judge, who meanwhile had kept on smoking a brass-bowled pipe, the stem of which was a yard long, while the bowl was only as big as a chestnut, asked,

"In what form did you say this evil magic came?"

At this, the miller's old father produced the box, opened it, and handed the metal mirror to the judge, who had never before seen anything like it. In fact, he had never been out of his district except once, when he went to the examinations, years before, in Seoul. Even then he was so much with his fellow students and so long shut up in his little cell writing out his essays that he saw hardly anything of the city.

When he held up the mirror before his eyes he suddenly became like a demon in his rage, and behaved just like the other people in the court-room.

On the face of the round thing which he held in his hand he saw a man in official robes, such as only men of eminence wear. He had on his head a high round hat, like those which only magistrates ever put on, while on his right ear hung a string of twenty-eight big round amber beads.

When he held the mirror down in front of him he discerned also the embroidered breastpiece, and the little silver stork, that served to hold together the folds of a judge's coat of office, while around his waist was a decorated girdle.

All this made him almost choke with anger, at the idea that another magistrate should come into the village of Cucumberville, to take his place.

What should he himself do for a salary? If he lost his position how would he support his old parents and his twenty-five poor relations? He saw himself a pauper in his old age.

Speechless with rage there was silence in the court-room for at least half a minute. Even the women's tongues did not wag. All looked at each other to see what would come next.

But the peace lasted no longer than thirty seconds, for the storm broke out again in full force when the jealous wife seized her husband by his topknot to drag him home. She feared that the magistrate was himself so angry and jealous, that he might adjourn the court.

Just when the hullaballoo was at its height, a messenger rushed into the court-room, to announce that the royal inspector direct from the king was on his travels of observation in the province. Within five minutes he would be at the gate of the court house.

Instantly the jealous wife let go her husband's topknot. The magistrate called for order and posted his under officers in their places, according to the etiquette of welcoming the king's agents. Then the magistrate adjusting his hat and topknot which had been badly tumbled in his passion went out to greet his worship, the Royal Inspector. Salutations over, he waved his hand to his superior to take to the chief seat of honor.

As soon as all formalities were over, the high officer inquired into the cause of the troubles and into the merits of the case.

The local magistrate put the mirror on a silken cushion and handed both to his highness, the inspector, saying:

"Please, your worship, it is this that has turned us all into devils of jealousy. What is it?"

Then this gentleman from the capital, who was every day accustomed to the comforts and conveniences of the great city and the splendor of the palace, explained what a mirror was. He gave them all a mild scolding for their folly and dismissed them, telling them that whenever he or she felt angry, or jealous, to go out and pull the tops off five turnips; or, to drink slowly a cup of rice water before speaking an angry word.

Thereupon, the miller's wife fell on her face and begged pardon of her husband. Then, all the family, young and old, while walking home, laughed heartily at their mistakes.

When a Korean begins to laugh, it is sometimes hard for him to stop; but after half an hour, all was quiet again. After that, nearly every one who could afford it bought a mirror. All the girls in the village, sooner or later, possessed one.

They used to look into its face so often to see their own, that the oiled-paper carpet fronting the mirror was, in many houses, soon worn out.

In Seoul, the mirror-makers wondered what had happened in Cucumberville, the village, so long famous only for its cucumbers, but they slapped their thighs for joy and grew rich.

OLD TIMBER TOP

The fairies in the Korean province of Kang Wen, which means River Meadow, were having great fun, when one of their number told how they played a trick on an ox-driver whom they called Old Timber Top. How he got such a strange name this story will tell.

This driver was a rich and stingy fellow who had made a fortune in lumber. He used to buy up all the trees he could. Then he would have them cut down and sawed up into logs and boards. His men would haul them away in their rough carts, drawn by stout bulls, to his lumber yard. In winter time sleds were used, but whether it was the season of snow and ice, or of tree blossoms and flowers, the animal used to draw sleds or carts was always a bull.

For in Korea, horses or donkeys do not know how to pull anything. The ponies and donkeys are too small. Not being used to the work, if harnessed they would kick the wagon all to pieces.

They can carry loads on their backs, but the bulls can do this also, so the creature with horns is considered to be the most valuable of beasts of burden. Besides, he fills the purse and makes good dinners when his owner is through with him.

You can see these patient carriers loaded with brushwood or sticks piled so high they seem to be carrying small mountains of twigs, grass and leaves for kindlings, or with heavy logs of wood for fuel. Yet when the bull is very young, a mere baby, he has a happier time than a colt or little donkey, for he lives in the house and is the children's pet.

Old Timber Top sold his logs and boards at such high prices that the poor suffered. This was because they were cold and could not afford to pay so many strings of cash for fuel. The people used to say that the old fellow would skin a mosquito for his hide and tallow. So sometimes they gave him the nickname of Skin-flay.

Not many of the villagers were able to buy planks of wood thick and heavy and strong enough to keep their pigs from the tigers, which came down from the mountains and prowled about at night in the villages. These long-haired and black-striped beasts got to be so fond of pork, that even in the snow they would, without fearing the cold or the guns of the hunters, claw up the tops of the pens and get down among the squealing prey. They might get a baby pig at once or perhaps drag out and carry off enough of a big pork to feed their cubs for a week. All the stables and cow-houses had to be made very strong, for the tigers, when they had gone a good while without food, seemed to be hungry enough to eat a horse with all his harness on, and even a grown-up cow or ox. Yet as a rule, no tiger cared to taste either beef or horse meat, if he could get young pork or veal.

Old Timber Top was not satisfied to make money at his lumber yard only. It is the custom in Korea to plant the most beautiful trees around tombs or in the cemeteries. When this skin-flint heard of a family which had become so poor that they must needs sell the splendid trees which had been planted around their ancestors' graves he sent his agents to buy the timber. These fellows would load up a horse with long ropes, of copper and iron cash, coins that had a square hole in the middle and were strung together with twine made of twisted straw. It was a heavy horse load to carry twenty dollars' worth of coin. Arrived on the spot, after beating the owner down to the lowest price possible, Old Timber Top's men would go out, chop down and saw up the grand trees, leaving only the sawdust on the graves, while the people wept to lose what they loved.

In this way the landscape was spoiled and this made many villagers very angry at such a man, for the Koreans love natural scenery and almost worship fine trees, which had made the country beautiful for centuries.

But what cared Old Timber Top, provided he could pile up his strings of cash and jingle his silver?

In time, this hard old fellow could think of nothing else but how to get richer out of the wants and sufferings of other people. The wealthier he became, the more he wanted. Yet he did not get any happier. Nobody loved him, while many hated him.

At last he thought he would make a trip to Seoul, the great capital city, which every Korean hopes to see sometime. There he expected to receive honor and appointment to rank and office. Timber Top had a relative who was high in the king's service, who, he thought, would assist him; for all Koreans are kind and helpful to each other, especially when they are related.

To be an officer Timber Top knew would permit him, even to wear a gorgeously shining mandarin's hat with wide flaps or wings on it and a long white silk coat with a big square on the breast of velvet or satin, embroidered with storks or dragons, clouds and waves. When he went out on the streets he could strut about, as if he were the lord of the universe; for he would then wear a hat so high and with such a round wide brim, that he would not dare to go out during a high wind, for fear of being blown away, like a ship in a tempest. In such a costume he would be saluted by servants and the common people, who would bow down before him, because they would think him a great man.

But how could he win such a position and gain the glory of it?

He was not a scholar, learned in books, or in law, or a doctor of medicine. Not being a soldier, either, he knew nothing of war. He could not ride on a monocycle, as a general did, drawn or pushed by four men and dressed in a long red coat studded all over with shining metal with a brass helmet on his head, on the top of which was a little dragon. He feared, even if he were appointed, he might fall off the one-wheeled vehicle and show what a fool he was.

Nevertheless this old fellow was so vain and full of conceit that he followed what was once the common custom in Korea. He took his journey to Seoul, leaving his family behind him to live on the cheapest kind of kimchi, with turnips and millet.

Now the Koreans are all famous for giving welcome and showing hospitality to their poor relations, and often they do this even to tramps and lazy people. When a man becomes rich or holds a high office, he usually has around him many hangers on. Some, we should even say, were loafers.

So on arriving in Seoul, Old Timber Top took up his quarters in one part of his relative's big house. There he lived a long time and was treated decently, for he always was saying soft things and making flattering speeches to his host. In fact, he bowed down like a slave when in presence of his august master. Yet, in truth, he was despised even by the servants and work people.

In order not to wear his welcome entirely out he had to make from time to time a handsome present to his patron. This steadily reduced both his income and his fortune, and while these were shrinking his family at home suffered, so that, by and by, he received notice by letter that his business had dried up and soon no more money could be sent to him in Seoul. While he lingered news from home grew worse and worse. His wife was obliged to sell their house to pay debts. The next item was that she and her daughter were living in a wretched shanty at the end of the village and were no longer in society.

All this time those in Seoul who knew that the foolish fellow was as ambitious as ever to wear the fine white clothes of a scholar, or the gay colors of a soldier, declared that Old Timber Top had no brains. They even jested about a pumpkin set on shoulders, or they laughed when they declared that the wood, which he had sold so long, had gone to his head. They debated in the wine shops whether, if his skull were opened, pumpkin seeds or timber would be found inside of it.

So they, also, called him "Old Timber Top," meaning that inside his skull was a wooden head and no better than that of an idol carved out of persimmon wood, such as were so plentiful in the Buddhist temples. Others declared that he had a real head of bone and brains, but "he carried it under his arm pits," as the saying was.

When the fairies heard all this, they unanimously resolved to reform the old fellow, even if they had to make an ox of him.

Timber Top, now poor and bankrupt, knew he must leave Seoul and go home and work for a living. When he made his final call on his rich Seoul relative and told him he must, to his great regret, take his leave and go back to his native village, he was not well received. Being too poor to buy a present to give to his host, on whose bounty he had lived so long, he was answered coldly and told to go and do as he liked.

And this, after years of fawning and gift-making! Not a word of thanks or appreciation! Poor Timber Top was down in the mouth and his heart was cold in his bosom. He knocked on his head with his fists, to find out whether, after all, it had really turned into timber.

On his way back, a big storm came on and when he came to a village inn, cold, wet and hungry, he begged for shelter over night. The woman who kept it was the wife of a butcher, who was then away from home. This was an awful blow to Timber Top's pride, for butchers were held to be the lowest of people, and they were not even allowed to wear hats, like the rest of the men in Korea.

The woman was kind to the traveler. She gave him a hot supper and let him sleep in that room of the house which had the best stone floor, under which the flues from the kitchen fire ran. So he warmed himself and baked his clothes, which were sopping wet, until they were dry. He was so tired that he kept on sleeping till very late next morning, and nearly to the noon hour. He was altogether so comfortable that to him it seemed as if he were a great man in the capital, thus to receive such kind treatment.

Waking up from one of his naps, he heard what he thought was the big butcher, who had come home, asking of his wife in a gruff tone of voice, "Where is that ox? I must sell him this morning, for it is market day," he said.

In less than a minute more, the man and his wife entered the room with four sticks which the fairies had put there, a halter, and a rope, made of twisted rice straw, besides a thick iron ring, such as they put into bulls' noses, to make them obey their masters. Throwing down the iron ring and rope on the floor, in a trice they had thrust the stick under Old Timber Top's back. In a moment more, he felt horns growing out of his head, and his lips becoming thick as sausages. His mouth was as wide as a saucer and had big teeth growing on the upper jaw. A tail sprouted at his other end and the four sticks became four legs.

Before he could quite understand just what was going on, or what the matter could be, Old Timber Top was standing on four legs and the butcher was slipping the ring through his nose. Oh how it did hurt!

It was an awkward job to get the animal out of the room and through the narrow door, and some of the paper on the walls and the furniture suffered. But finally when out in the open air the bull, that was no other than what had been the man Timber Top, went quietly along to the market place. Any attempt to pull his head away, or to stop or run off, or in any way to misbehave, hurt his nose so dreadfully, that he quickly quit. The butcher needed to give only a slight jerk of the rope when the bull changed his gait and was as quiet as a lamb, even though as an animal he was big enough to gore the man and toss him on its horns, or crush him by trampling on him with his hoofs, if once he got angry.

One would have supposed that Timber Top would be a fighting bull, but no! In the market place he stood patiently and quietly for hours, hardly even stamping, when the flies began to bite.

"Oh that I had been as diligent and kept on at my honest occupation in my native village, as that fly!" mused the bull, that still had a man's memory.

At last there came a man with money to buy. He was a drover, who unloaded his pony and paid down many strings, or about twenty pounds, of copper and iron cash. The owner put the halter in the buyer's hand, and the new master then led off Timber Top to be sold to a butcher who lived up in his home town in the north. This fellow intended first to fatten the animal and then turn him into steaks and stewing meat.

But on his way the new owner thought that, because he had made a good bargain, he must stop at a wine shop and have a drink. So he tied Timber Top's nose with the rope to the low wall, which enclosed a turnip field, and went inside the shop.

But while the drover's wine went in his wits went out, and he fell asleep and stayed in the shop a long time. In fact, it was as the old song said:

> "First the man takes a dram,
> Then the dram takes another dram;
> Then the dram takes the man."

Meanwhile Timber Top looked over the low wall, and, yielding to temptation, pulled up with his teeth some of the plants by the roots, first chewing the green leaves and then grinding the turnips and swallowing them.

Presto! The horns drew in and shrivelled up. The ring dropped out of his nose and fell with a crash on the stones of the village path. His two forelegs turned into arms, the hair and hoofs became human legs and Old Timber Top was a man, and himself once again. To make sure of it he felt himself all over; pulled his own nose, felt around his back to see if he had a tail, and rubbed his head for horns. None there! He looked down and found he had only two legs. Then he swung his arms with delight, at being once more a man.

"Well named, Turn-up thou," he mused, "thou green plant with a mustard-like taste. Thou hast turned me inside out. Or, have the fairies been busy?"

He had hardly got these ideas through his half wooden head, that he was on two legs and a man once more and could think like one, than he started on the road home. Just then the drover rushed out of the wine shop and accosted him, saying:

"Have you seen a stray bull anywhere near this place?"

Of course Timber Top using fine language, like a yang ban, said there was no bull in the neighborhood that he could see or knew of, and he had heard none bellowing. Then he gave the drover a look of contempt for being so stupid, and for asking of him, a gentleman, so foolish a question.

Yet after he was out of sight of the drover he slapped his thighs, as Koreans do when they are amused at their own smartness, and went on joyfully. He kept on repeating to himself, "sticks and turnips, turnips and sticks."

Then a big idea struck him, as if it were a tap on a wooden drum, such as one sees in Buddhist temples. It hit his brain so hard and so swelled his head, that his big Korean hat nearly toppled off. Immediately he put this idea into action.

He returned hastily to the inn and into the room in which he had been turned into a bull and stole the butcher's four fairy sticks, which stood in a corner, then he hied at once over the roads towards the capital.

Reaching Seoul, he went to the house of his rich relative, where he had waited ten years for the fortune and the favor which did not come. Going into his host's bedroom, he tapped the high lord of the house with the fairy sticks, not hard, but only lightly.

Forthwith the man's head became horns at the top, with muzzle of thick lips in front. His hands turned into front hoofs and his legs into the hind quarters of a bull. Yet he was not entirely an ox, but only half animal and half man.

Old Timber Top stopped tapping and then went away, to await events, leaving the creature half man and half ox. He knew that soon he would be called in.

When the family of wife, many sons, several daughters, servants, retainers, hangers-on, and what not, saw their master half man and half ox, with horns and hoofs, they were distracted. Each one had his own notion of how to get him back into human form and like his former self. Each one ran all over town and into the adjoining villages to get and call in the mudangs.

These mudangs were the people, mostly women, whose business it was to drive out the imps and bad fairies, such as had, in this case, done the mischief. The kitchen maids stoutly declared that Tokgabi had wrought the change upon their master. They felt quite sure of it; but the men thought that the gods of the mountains were punishing him for his sins. On the other hand, the mudang woman said she would find out and get him back into his human skin, if they paid her enough money.

With drums and dancing and songs, screams, yells, and every sort of noise, the mudangs kept up such a terrible racket that it almost deafened the family. There were several of them called in, and they knew that they would all be well paid.

Meanwhile the doctors also kept on with their awful medicines, besides rubbing, pounding, blowing, and sticking needles into the bull and burning moxa, or little balls of cottony mugwort, on its hide.

Yet not a hoof or horn, not even a hair changed.

The mudangs declared that the imps had got inside the man and they must get them out. One fellow carried a big bottle to trap the imps and cork them in. Another insisted that they would have to use scissors and snip the skin in about a hundred places, thus making small holes to let the evil creatures out. Then they must bottle them up, lest they should get out and overrun the house and infest the whole town.

There seemed not so many chances of getting well as "one hair among nine oxen"; but the wife pleaded that they would put off using the scissors until all other means had failed. She did not want to see her dear husband's skin made into a colander, or sieve, if it could be helped.

At this point, when the din and the despair were worst and had come to a climax, Old Timber Top appeared. As some of the family had collapsed and lay helpless on the floor, and as all were too tired to ask questions, they at once made way for him. After looking at the patient with a face as wise as an owl's, Old Timber Top solemnly announced that only one thing could save him and that was a rare and wonderful drug, of which only he knew the secret, but which he could speedily procure. Of course the wife, sons and daughters instantly promised to give up their all, to see their husband and father himself again.

So while Timber Top went out to get the famous medicine, they all fell asleep, tired out, while the ox-man lay over on his side resting his horns and hoofs on the floor bed; for in Korea they do not have bedsteads, that is, beds raised up from the floor.

As for Old Timber Top, when once out on the street, he immediately began saying to himself, over and over again, "Turnips and sticks, sticks and turnips."

Going to a vegetable shop, he bought a fine large turnip, or turnip-radish, of the kind that grows in Korea, silvery white and about four feet long. He first peeled, then sliced, and finally pounded it into a sauce very fine. Then entering the house in triumph, he woke up the doctors, kicked the servants awake, and announced that the potent drug would soon restore their master. He solemnly bade them all watch and see him do it.

Pulling and hauling all together, five or six fellows were able to get the man-bull on his two hoofs and two feet and then Timber Top put a spoonful of the sauce on the big tongue.

At once a most marvellous change took place!

The horns shortened until they disappeared, the lips thinned, the mouth became smaller. Hoofs, hair, and hide departed into empty air. In the wagging of a dog's tail, the mighty man of the house had become himself again.

All the doctors, jugglers, and mudangs packed up their imp-bottles and medicines, and with their drums, flutes, bags, boxes and wares slunk away, while the family loaded Old Timber Top with grateful thanks and compliments.

As for the master, he declared Timber Top the greatest physician the world ever knew. He invited him to make the house his permanent home and showered upon him many gifts, with plenty to eat, and white clothes starched as white as snow. The hats with which he presented Timber Top were so big around and had a brim so wide, that he used them when covered with oiled paper covers as umbrellas in rainy weather, but he never went out doors when the wind was blowing, for fear he would be whirled down the street. Besides this, he feared there was still much wood in his head, which might turn into a top and spin round, if he were not careful.

Old Timber Top set up a medicine office, practiced among the nobility and became physician to the king. When he visited the palace, he used a red visiting card, a foot long. He had a plastron, or square of velvet embroidery on his breast. He wore a string of amber beads as big as walnuts over his ears. He soon became fat with a double chin and plump fingers, showing that he reeked with prosperity. He lived to a good old age, his family were made comfortable, his sons and daughters married well, and he had seventeen grandchildren before he died.

Yet all the time, the fairies claimed that they did it all. They made the sticks work one way, and the turnips another, and they still play their tricks on the Koreans, especially those with more or less wood in their heads.

SIR ONE LONG BODY AND MADAM THOUSAND FEET

In the land of Morning Radiance, where the family names have only one syllable, such as Kim, Yi, Pil, Wun, Hap, etc., they wear shoes, but these are not made of black leather. The people neither stand up on wooden clogs as in Japan, nor case their feet in straight soled gaiters, without heels, as in China. The gentlemen put on white socks with tough hide soles, and the ladies don dainty slippers with the pointed toes turned up. Common folks' sandals are made chiefly of straw and twine and it takes a good deal of cordage to complete a pair.

Now there once lived under an old stone below a persimmon tree a fair young creature named Miss Thousand Feet. She wore lead-colored clothes and had so many toes to take care of that any one who tried to count them soon got tired; so he stopped and called the whole amount a thousand, which was a number as round as herself. She was as proud of each one of her many little feet as a Chinese lady, who has only two of them. Miss Thousand Feet was very modest, however, and if any one stepped on her toes, or touched her, she curled up, first into a ring and then into a ball, so that men, by a pun on her family name, called her "a pill millipede," for she belonged to the Pil family, one of the most famous in all Korea.

Miss Thousand Feet was very happy living under a damp stone in the cool earth and she played a good deal. But by and by, when she grew up, her parents told her it was time for her to get married. So they looked around, to see if any gentleman in the whole creation was worthy of her, not only to make a suitable husband, but also a good match.

Now in another village lived a rich, fat, young and promising male creature, named Mr. Long Body, of the Wum family. His business was to eat his way through the ground, and pile up little curled heaps of mud on the surface, and at this work he was kept very busy. He had to look out for the birds, for they enjoyed eating folks like him, he was so soft and sweet.

Constant exercise in moving through the ground kept his body shining, so that altogether, as earthworms go, he was quite handsome and considered a good catch for Miss Thousand Feet. Furthermore, as he had no feet and she had so many, while his body was long and hers quite short, it was supposed that one would make up where the other lacked and that both would be happy together as husband and wife.

Mr. Long Body, when he heard of the charms of Miss Thousand Feet, was of the same opinion. All his friends were pairing off, the males bringing home their brides to their fathers' houses and setting up housekeeping. As he had come of age, he also determined to marry.

So he sent letters and opened the business, according to Korean etiquette, through a "go-between," as the lady who arranges marriages is called. This person goes to see each of the two families, praising to one the beauty and graces of the promised bride and to the other the strength and wealth of the future husband. Indeed, she gives both of them a very good character. Finally the "six proprieties," or "half dozen rules," had been completed and the engagement of Mr. Wum and Miss Pil was announced.

What a clatter of gossip was at once heard in both villages! No one ever thought that such a handsome fellow as Mr. Long Body Wum would ever marry into the Pil family. Some jealous folks hinted that Mr. Long Body, if he took a wife with a thousand feet, would never be able to pay his shoemaker. On the other hand, so long as his bride would be content with plain twine shoes all might go well; but for extra occasions, or if his wife were extravagant and wanted lady's turned up house foot-gear made of red morocco such as only the rich folks wear,- well there would be trouble in the household. How *could* he keep her in shoes? Other persons, however, who knew that the Pils were famous people, wondered how Mr. Wum ever managed to get such a prize as Miss Pil.

In the other village, the tongues of the gossips ran on in much the same way. What did she see to admire in that fellow without legs? When the honeymoon would be over and it came to making gentleman's clothes for her husband, had she any skill with the needle? Could she make a long coat and one trouser leg big enough to fit him? And think of the many days of work necessary to cut and sew the garment, to say nothing of weary hours to be spent in washing, starching and giving a gloss to such clothes. The idea! Why, she would have to be nothing but a slave.

As her husband's semptress, tailor, and laundress she would get no rest. Think of washing, starching, and beating to a fine gloss the one-legged trousers, which Mr. Wum would often have to change; for he lived in the dirt!

Now, Mr. Long Body Wum was so busy with his work of excavating the ground that he had no time to pay attention to the village chatterboxes. Miss Pil, however, couldn't help hearing what the women and others said about her, and especially the talk concerning the terribly hard duties that awaited her if she took a husband. While Mr. Wum kept digging at the tunnel three yards long, which he was excavating underground, so as to save up and be ready for his wedding, Miss Pil brooded over what the gossips talked about and over those awfully long coats and one-legged trousers she would be obliged to sit up at nights to make, wash, starch and gloss. Already she imagined her arms tired in anticipation of starching and beating on the Korean lustre, without which no gentleman in the Land of Morning Calm ever goes outdoors. If his coat didn't have that fashionable shine which long beating gives, the women would notice it immediately and pretty soon the men also.

Miss Pil's broodings night and day over the matter did not help affairs, and finally wore upon her nerves. She refused to prepare her own trousseau, and despite all her friends told her in praise of Mr. Long Body Wum, she decided to write a letter to him, telling him that on account of his long trunk without limbs, and the great labor necessary to make him proper clothing and of starching and glossing it, to say nothing of keeping it in order, she felt unable to hold to the marriage engagement and must break it off.

But before she had dropped the water on the ink stone and begun to rub up the ink, or taken brush-pen and paper in hand,

Mr. Long Body had got wind of her complaining and it worried him. Why should he marry one who didn't want him?

Then, as he thought it over, being a very thrifty and economical bachelor, be began to doubt whether he could buy shoes enough to fit all the feet of his betrothed. He had not looked on her face or figure yet. Indeed it was hardly Korean etiquette that he should- openly at least. So far, he had not seen her tiny feet to count them up, but he suspected that, since she belonged to the Pil family, she must have a thousand feet according to her reputation. When he came to calculate what it would cost him, even in cheap twine sandals, he was startled. When he figured out what ladies' turned up kids would come to he was so alarmed that he nearly fainted. At the sight of five hundred pairs of shoes, however tiny, his breath almost failed him and he saw himself ruined. What should he do?

And when she took off her foot-gear at night, where should he stow it away? Then, what a noise she would make, if she put on rough-soled shoes, while at her work around the house and yard. It was horrible for a quiet bachelor even to think of the clatter she would make. Already he felt deafness coming on. Should he break off the engagement? Yet how could any one of the Wum family honorably do such a thing? What would the neighbors say? Could he, if prone to breaking his word, get another bride of a family so respectable as that of the Pil?

However he would sleep over it, as there were some days before the wedding. But next morning the matter cleared up, and he was able to crawl into his hole and out of sight with comfort. He sent a letter to Miss Pil, setting forth the facts, and asking for a release from the engagement to marry. The substance of what he wrote was this; that owing to his small fortune he would be unable to buy her all the shoes, and of the kind which a lady of her quality and tastes required. He therefore could not think of asking her to share his poverty, but begged her to secure another husband who could do so.

Now it happened that the letters crossed on the road. Each had a refusal before the ink was dry; so neither could complain.

So there was no wedding, nor any frolic among the young folks, or feasting of relatives, and to this day Miss Pil remains single and Mr. Wum has no wife. They were very severe on the girl. All the gossips say that it served the thousand-footed hussy right. Folks had better look on the good points in a person's character and not dwell upon his faults and defects. On the other hand, in Mr. Wum's village, all declare with one voice that bachelors should count up *all* the expense in getting married. Miss Pil still goes shoeless hiding from light under a stone, and Mr. Wum keeps out of sight underground, for he has nothing to wear.

THE SKY BRIDGE OF BIRDS

No bird is more common in Korea than the magpie. They are numbered by millions. Every day in the year, except the seventh day of the seventh month, the air is full of them. On that date, however, they have a standing engagement every year. They are all expected to be away from streets and houses, for every well-bred magpie is then far up in the sky building a bridge across the River of Stars, called the Milky Way. With their wings for the cables, and their heads to form the floor of the bridge, they make a pathway for lovers on either side of the Silver Stream.

Boys and girls are usually very kind to the magpies, but if a single one be found about the houses, on the roofs, or in the streets on the seventh of August, woe betide it! Every dirty-faced brat throws sticks or stones at the poor creature, for not being about its business of bridge-building across the Starry River. By evening time the magpies return to their usual places, for they are then supposed to have attended to their tasks and built the bridge.

To prove beyond a doubt that the bridge was made and walked over, you have only to look at the bare heads of the magpies at this time. Their feathers have been entirely worn off by the tramping of the crowd of retainers who follow the Prince of Star Land across the bridge to meet his bride.

If it be wet weather on the morning of this day of the Weaver Maiden and the Cattle Prince, the rain-drops are the tears of joy shed by the lovers at their first meeting. If showers fall in the afternoon, they are the tears of sadness at saying farewell, when the prince and princess leave each other. If any thunder is heard, every boy and girl knows that this comes from the rumble of the wagons which carry the baggage of the prince and princess, as they move away, each from the other, homeward.

Now, this is the story which the Korean mothers tell to their children of the Bridge of Birds.

Long, long ago, in the Kingdom of the Stars, a king reigned who had a lovely daughter. Besides being the most beautiful

to behold, she was a skilful weaver. There was no good thing to be done in the palace, but she could do it. She was not only highly accomplished, but of sweet temper and very willing. Being a model of all diligence, she was very greatly beloved of her parents and her influence over her father was very great. He would do almost anything to please his darling daughter.

In due time a young and very handsome prince, who lived in Star Land, came to her father's court and fell in love with the pretty princess. Her parents consenting, the wedding was celebrated with great splendor.

Now that she was a wife and had a home of her own to care for, she became all the more a model of lovely womanhood and an example to all the maidens of Korea forever. Besides showing diligence in the care of clothes and food and in setting her servants a good example of thrift, she thought much of their happiness. Her service to her husband was unremitting. Her chief ambition was to make his life one of constant joy.

But the prince, instead of following his bride's good example, and of appreciating what his beautiful and unselfish bride was doing for his happiness, gave himself up to waste and extravagance. He became lazy and dissipated. Neglecting his duties, he wasted his own fortune and his wife's dowry. He sold all his oxen and calves to get money only to lose it in gambling. He borrowed many and long ropes of coin from any one who would lend him the brass and iron money. Finally he was so scandalously poor, being on his last string of cash, that he was in danger of being degraded from his rank as prince, and of having his name spoken with contempt.

The King of the Stars, having seen his son-in-law on the downward way, had more than once threatened to disinherit, or banish him, especially after the prince had parted with his cattle. Yet when his daughter, the young wife, interceded and begged pardon for her husband, the king relented, paid his son-in-law's debts and gave him another chance to do better. When, however, the worthless fellow fell back into his old ways, and grew worse and worse, the king resolved to separate the pair, one from the other. He banished the prince, far, far away, six months' distance from the north side of the River of Heaven, and exiled the princess a half year's measure of space from the south side of the Starry Stream.

Although the king in his wrath had hardened his heart, even against his own beloved child, and had driven her from court and palace, because of her worthless husband, yet, as a signal proof of his compassion, he ordained that on one night of the year, on the seventh night of the seventh moon, they might meet for a few hours.

The young people parted and took their sad journey to the edge of the starry heavens, but they loved each other so dearly that, as soon as they arrived at their place of banishment, they turned round to meet each other on August th.

So when the day came, after six months' weary journeying, they had reached the edge of the Starry River, and there they stood, catching glimpses and waving their hands, but unable to get closer to each other. There one may see them on summer nights shining on opposite sides of the broad Stream of Stars, loving each other but unable to cross.

Feeling that the great gulf of space could not be spanned, the loving couple burst into tears. The flood from their eyes, making the river overflow, deluged the earth below, threatening to float everything, houses, people, animals away. What could be done?

The four-footed creatures, fish and fowls, held a convention, but it was agreed that only those birds with strong wings and able to fly high could do anything. So the magpies, with many flattering speeches, were commended to the enterprise.

When these noisy and chattering creatures, that are nevertheless so kind and friendly to the sparrows, heard of the lovers' troubles aloft, they resolved to help the sorrowing pair over the River of Stars. Out of their big, ugly nests they flew gladly to the convention that voted to build the bridge. Sending out word all over the world, millions of magpies assembled in the air. Under the direction of their wisest chiefs, they began their work of making, with a mass of wings, a flying bridge that would reach from shore to shore of the Starry Stream. First, they put their heads together to furnish a floor, and, so closely, that the bridge looked as if it were paved with white granite. Then with their pinions they held up the great arch and highway, over which the prince crossed to his bride with all his baggage and train of followers. The tables were soon spread and the two royal lovers enjoyed a feast, with many tender words and caresses.

Every year, for ages past, on the seventh day of the seventh month, the magpies have done this. Indeed, although the star lovers meet only once a year, yet as they live on forever the wife has her husband and the husband his wife much longer than mortal couples who live on earth. It is law in the magpie kingdom that no bird can shirk this work.

Any magpie that tries to get out of the task and that is too bad or lazy to do its part in bridge building, is chased away by the Korean children, who want no such truant around. For does not every girl hope to be as diligent and accomplished as the Star Princess, so that when she grows up she may make as good a wife as the lovely lady that every year stands by the Starry River to meet her lord? As for the boys, it is hoped that they will become as faithful husbands as the penitent bridegroom, who every year, on the night of August th, awaits his bride on the shining shore of the River of Stars.

LONGKA, THE DANCING GIRL

After the islanders in the Eastern Ocean had found out how rich Korea was, they were not satisfied with their own land. They seemed to have eyes like dragon flies, that wanted everything they saw. They kept on borrowing until they got many of the plants and animals which they now possess, which as everybody knows came from the Land of Morning Glory.

Even the neko, or Korean cat, was carried over to the islands; though in some way it lost its tail on the voyage or else had it bobbed. This is the reason why poor pussy in these islands seems to carry around with her something like a corkscrew, instead of a tail. Moreover, when the Korean puss, that had so long been accustomed to scrambling over the roofs and back alleys at home, was introduced into the islands, it was thought to be a wild animal, and for a long time was treated as a fox or badger would be. However, because it kept down the rats and the mice this bob-tailed puss was highly valued.

Yet not content with borrowing so many things, the greedy islemen thought they might as well have all Korea and everything in it, and then go further and overrun China.

So they sent a great army in a mighty fleet of ships to invade the Koreans' country. They took horses with them, but as their soldiers were fed chiefly on rice, salt fish and pickles, they did not need any wagons. They had only oxen to draw their carts, for they had never trained horses to pull anything, but only to be pack and saddle animals.

This army of islanders marched to the capital, in which were palaces, and pagodas. Then they sent one of their armies along the sea front and another along the west coast. They expected to march into China, but two things happened to prevent this. So, after they had wasted and tarried in the country for five years, they gave it up and were sent home flying.

From the north a Chinese army came to the help of the Koreans and drove the islemen to the coast. But when they got there they found their ships were gone. A clever Korean admiral had invented an iron-clad ship that rammed and sunk their war junks. So their army had to wait till a new fleet of ships had been built and then came over to take them back.

But before the islanders left Korea they smashed statues and monuments, broke up images and even the observatories for the study of the stars. They took marble pagodas apart to load on their ships and carry away. They enticed, or forced to go with them, hundreds of the Korean potters, artists, and craftsmen.

For, by this time, the islanders had given up living in huts of straw and roving about like Arabs or gypsies. They had cities with paved streets, like as in Korea, though they had none of the beautiful marble pagodas and images and temples, for everything was of wood, while thousands of large buildings and images in Korea were of stone, chiseled into beautiful forms.

Now in Korea there were some beautiful daughters of the land and many noblemen and men of courage, who determined not to be carried away from their dearly beloved country. Of this, in southern Korea, the Rock of the Fallen Flower is to this day the witness.

Over three hundred years ago, when "the terrible fighting dwarfs," as the Koreans called their enemies, came, they encamped in a town where lived a beautiful dancing girl named Longka. Being a ge-sang, (gei-sha) or accomplished young lady, she could sing beautifully. The islanders took this lovely damsel prisoner and made her a waitress in the general's tent.

One night a great banquet was given in a famous pleasure hall named the Cliff House, because it was built on the high bank overlooking a deep river. All the chief captains were invited and the large room was illuminated with a thousand wax lights. These were tall and square candles, moulded into a beautiful shape, and each one was painted and decorated with figures of flowers, birds and pet animals. Very odd and ornamental is a Korean candle.

O how charming was the dancer, and what a beautiful sight to behold, was her graceful posing! For, Korean dances tell stories of birds and flowers, of summer, and of lovely snow-covered landscapes in winter, of a boat in a storm, of a tiger in a trap, of a brave soldier in battle, or a sad lady in the palace, or of the fairy tales of the Western Queen Mother and many others. Those who watch the dance and know the manners and customs, the dancer's gestures and poses, the motions of her fan and sleeves, besides the games of the children, the sports of the people, the harvest songs and the fun at the festivals, can read, because they see, the story of each told in most graceful motions. There are several languages, besides words which are spoken, and these appeal to the eye, instead of the ear.

The pretty dancer was robed in pure white, with ermine-edged slippers, and jeweled girdle, and her shining hair was done up like a queen's. Loud was the applause among the spectators at the end of every dance.

After the dinner was over, the general of the islanders grew very lively, because he had drunk much wine, and was not satisfied to see the dances of the lovely girl. Some of the rude soldiers also wanted to waltz with the beautiful maiden. But it was not the custom for Korean virgins to dance, or waltz, with male partners; for in this Country of Gentle Manners, dancing is by the sexes apart.

Yet the rough islanders insisted and forced her so hard, that she felt that both her own modesty and her country were outraged. She thought of the thousands of her countrymen, brothers, fathers and friends, who had died on the battle field, in defending their beloved land. Why should not she? So, pretending to yield to her country's enemies, she drew the general out of the banqueting hall and down toward the river, close to the edge of the rock.

Before he knew her purpose she seized his hands and leaped out, dragging her enemy with her over the cliff, and both passed into the other world.

She died for her country. To this day, the Rock of the Falling Flower is pointed out, and the story is told that here was exhibited a woman's devotion to her country. Around this rock poets have entwined their verses, while romantic associations cluster like the azalea flowers, that cover the hills of Korea with a riot of color, making their land seem to the natives the most beautiful on earth.

A FROG FOR A HUSBAND

Off in a valley among very stony mountains, lived an old farmer named Pak We and his wife. His land was poor and he had to toil from sunrise to sunset and often in the night, when the moon was shining, to get food. No child had ever come to his home and he was in too great straits of poverty to adopt a son. So he took his amusement in fishing in the pond higher up on the hills, that fed the stream which watered his millet and rice fields. Being very skilful he often caught a good string of fish and these he sold in the village near by to get for himself and his wife the few comforts they needed. Thus the old couple kept themselves happy, despite their cheerless life, though they often wondered what would become of them when they got too old to work.

But one summer Pak noticed that there were fewer fish in the pond and that every day they seemed to be less in number. Where he used to catch a stringful in an hour, he could hardly get half that many during a whole day.

What was the matter? Was he getting less skilful? Was the bait poor?

Not at all! His worms were as fat, his hooks and lines in as good order, and his eyesight was as keen as ever.

When Pak noticed also that the water was getting shallower, he was startled. Could it be that the pond was drying up?

Things grew worse day by day until at last there were no fish.

Where once sparkled the wavelets of a pond was now an arid waste of earth and stones, over which trickled hardly more than a narrow rill, which he could jump over. No fish and no pond meant no water for his rice fields. In horror at the idea of starving, or having to move away from his old home and become a pauper, Pak looked down from what had been the banks of the pond to find the cause of all this trouble. There in the mud among the pebbles he saw a bullfrog, nearly as big as an elephant, blinking at him with its huge round eyes.

In a rage the farmer Pak burst out, charging the frog with cruelty in eating up all the fish and drinking up all the water, threatening starvation to man and wife. Then Pak proceeded to curse the whole line of the frog's ancestors and relatives, especially in the female line, for eight generations back, as Koreans usually do.

But instead of being sorry, or showing any anger at such a scolding, the bullfrog only blinked and bowed, saying:

"Don't worry, Farmer Pak. You'll be glad of it, by and by. Besides, I want to go home with you and live in your house.

"What! Occupy my home, you clammy reptile! No you won't," said Pak.

"Oh! but I have news to tell you and you won't be sorry, for you see what I can do. Better take me in."

Old Pak thought it over. How should he face his wife with such a guest? But then, the frog had news to tell and that might please the old lady, who was fond of gossip. Since her husband was not very talkative, she might be willing to harbor so strange a guest.

So they started down the valley. Pak shuffled along as fast as his old shins could move, but the bullfrog covered the distance in a few leaps, for his hind legs were three feet long.

Arrived at his door, Mrs. Pak was horrified at the prospect of boarding such a guest. But when the husband told her that Froggie knew all about everybody and could chat interestingly by the hour, she changed her manner and bade him welcome. Indeed, she so warmed in friendliness that she gave him one of her best rooms. All the leaves, grass and brushwood that had been gathered in the wood-shed to supply the kitchen fire and house flues, was carried into the room. There it was doused with tubs of water to make a nice soft place such as bullfrogs like. After this he was fed all the worms he wanted.

Then after his dinner and a nap, Mrs. Pak and Mr. Pak donned their best clothes and went in to make a formal call on their guest.

Mr. Bullfrog was so affable and charming in conversation, besides telling so many good stories and serving up so many dainty bits of gossip, that Mrs. Pak was delighted beyond expression. Indeed, she felt almost like adopting Froggie as her son.

The night passed quietly away, but when the first rays of light appeared, Froggie was out on the porch singing a most melodious tune to the rising sun. When Mr. and Mrs. Pak rose up to greet their guest and to hear his song, they were amazed to find that the music was bringing them blessings. Everything they had wished for, during their whole lives, seemed now at hand, with more undreamed of coming in troops. In the yard stood oxen, donkeys and horses loaded with every kind of box, bale and bundle waiting to be unloaded and more were coming; stout men porters appeared and began to unpack, while troops of lovely girls in shining white took from the men's hands beautiful things made of jade, gold and silver. There were fine clothes and hats for Mr. Pak, jade-tipped hairpins, tortoise-shell and ivory combs, silk gowns, embroidered and jeweled girdles and every sort of frocks and woman's garments for Mrs. Pak, besides inlaid cabinets, clothes-racks and wardrobes. Above all, was a polished metal mirror that looked like the full autumn moon, over which Mrs. Pak was now tempted to spend every minute of her time.

Four or five of the prettiest maidens they had ever seen in all their lives danced, sang and played sweetest music. The unpacking of boxes, bales and bundles continued. Tables of jade and finest sandalwood were spread with the richest foods and wines. Soon, under the skilful hands of carpenters and decorators, instead of oiled paper on the floors, covering old bricks and broken flat stones set over the flues, and smoky rafters and mud walls poorly papered, there rose a new house. It had elegant wide halls, and large rooms with partitions made of choicest joiner work. It was furnished with growing flowers, game boards for chess and had everything in it like a palace. As for the riches of the larder and the good things to eat daily laid on the table, no pen but a Korean's can tell of them all. In the new storehouse were piles of dried fish, edible seaweed, bags of rice, bins of millet, tubs of kim-chi made of various sorts of the pepper-hash and Korean hot pickle in which the natives delight, to say nothing of peaches, pears, persimmons, chestnuts, honey, barley, sugar, candy, cake and pastry, all arranged in high piles and in gay colors.

The old couple seemed able to eat and enjoy twice as big dinners as formerly, for all the while the adopted Bullfrog was very entertaining. Mr. and Mrs. Pak laughed continually, declaring they had never heard such good stories as he told. The good wife was, however, quite equal to her guest in retailing gossip. One of her favorite subjects, of which she never tired, was the beauty and charm of Miss Peach. She was the accomplished daughter of the big Yang-ban, or nobleman, Mr. Poom, who lived in a great house, with a host of servants and retainers in the next village, and Mrs. Pak insisted there was no young woman in the world like her. It was noticed that Mr. Bullfrog was particularly interested when Miss Peach Poom was the subject of the old lady's praises.

After a week of such luxury, during which Mr. and Mrs. Pak seemed to dwell in the Nirvana, or Paradise, which the good priests often talked about, Mr. Pak's full cup of joy was dashed to earth when the Bullfrog informed him that he intended to marry, and that Mr. Pak must get him a wife. Still worse than that, Pak was informed by the Frog that he would have no one but Miss Peach, the daughter of Poom, so renowned for her beauty and graces.

At this, old Pak went nearly wild. He begged to be excused from the task, but the Bullfrog was inexorable. So, after inprecating his wife's tongue, for her ever putting it into the frog's head to marry Miss Peach, he donned his fine clothes and set out to see Mr. Poom. He expected to be beaten to death for his brazen effrontery in asking a noble lady to marry a frog.

Now this Mr. Poom had long been the magistrate of a district, who had squeezed much money wrongly from the poor people over whom he ruled, and having won great wealth, had retired and come back to his native place to live. This man had two daughters married, but the third, the youngest and most beautiful, Miss Peach, was now eighteen years old.

Arriving at the Pooms' grand mansion, Mr. Pak told of the suitor's wealth, power and fame, high position and promise, and how he had made the old couple happy.

Old Poom had pricked up his ears from the first mention of riches and power, and became highly interested as Pak went on sounding the praises of his prospective son-in-law.

"And what is his name?" asked Mr. Poom.

Here Pak was in a quandary. He knew that the frog family was the oldest and most numerous in the world and was famous for fine voices. He fell into a brown study for a few minutes. Then, looking up he declared that he had so long thought of the suitor's graces and accomplishments, that he had forgotten his name and could not then recall it.

So Mr. Poom, in order to help Pak out, ran over the list of famous families in Korea, reciting the names of the Kims, Sims, Mins, the Hos, Chos, Kos, Quongs and Hongs, etc., etc., for Mr. Poom was an authority on the Korean peerage.

"It is none of these," said Pak. "I deeply regret that I cannot recall the name."

"Strange," said Mr. Poom. "I have named all the families of any standing in the kingdom. What is his office or rank and where do his relations live?"

Pak was pressed so hard by Mr. Poom's searching questions that at last he had to confess that the suitor for the beautiful maiden was not a man but a frog.

"What! do you want me to marry my daughter to a pond-croaker? You shall suffer for thus insulting me in my own house. Slaves, bring the cross-bench and give this wretch twenty blows."

Forthwith, while four men brought out the whipping bench, three others seized poor Pak, stripped off his coat, and bound him with feet and arms stretched out to the bench. Then a tall, stalwart fellow raised the huge paddle of wood to let fall with all his might on the bare flesh of the old man.

But all this while the sky was darkening, and, before the first blow was given, the lightning flashed, the thunder rolled, and floods of rain fell that threatened to overwhelm house, garden, and all in a deluge. The hail, which began to pelt the cattle, was first the size of an egg and then of stones, like cannon-balls.

"Hold," cried the frightened Mr. Poom. "I'll wait and ask further."

Thereupon the lightning and thunder ceased, the sun burst out in splendor.

Mightily impressed by this, Mr. Poom at last agreed to let his daughter become the bride of the frog, not telling her who her husband was to be. Within an hour, while she was getting ready, a string of fine horses and donkeys with palanquins loaded with presents for the bride and her family appeared. Besides boxes of silk dresses and perfumes, head-gear and articles for a lady's boudoir, there were troops of maidens to wait on the bride. Arraying Miss Peach in the loveliest of robes, they also dressed her hair, until, what with satin puffs and frame, jade-tipped silver hairpins, rosettes and flowers, her head-gear stood over a foot high above her forehead, on which was the bride's red round spot. Then when the happy maiden had sufficiently admired herself in the metal mirror and heard the praises of her attendant virgins, she entered the bridal palanquin- a gorgeous mass of splendor. According to custom, her eyes were sealed shut and covered with wax, for a Korean bride sees nothing of her husband until the end of the feast, when she meets him in the bridal chamber.

So to his house she was carried in great pomp and with gay attendance of brilliantly arrayed maidens. The marriage ceremony and the grand supper were happy affairs for all the guests, even though the bride, according to Korean etiquette, was as if blind, quietly and patiently waiting sightless throughout the whole joyful occasion. The actual ceremony was witnessed only by the foster-parents and the bridegroom.

When in the bridal chamber, the bride having unsealed her eyes, and her vision being clear, she looked up at the one she had married and found not a man, but a frog, she was furiously angry. She burst out into a protest against having such a bridegroom.

Gently and in tenderest tones the bridegroom attempted first to comfort her. Then, handing her a pair of scissors, he begged her to rip open the skin along his back from shoulder to thigh, for it was very tight and he was suffering pain from it.

In her bitter disappointment at being married to a frog, she seized the scissors and almost viciously began to cut from nape to waist. Her surprise was great to find what seemed to be silk underneath the speckled skin. When she had slit down two yards or so, her husband the frog stood upon his hind legs. He twisted himself about as if in a convulsion, pulled his whole speckled hide hard with his front paws, and then jumping out of his skin, stood before his bride a prince. Fair, tall, of superb figure, and gorgeously arrayed, he was the ideal of her dreams. A jeweled baldric bound his waist, embroidery of golden dragons on his shoulders and breast told of his rank, while on his head was the cap of royalty with a sparkling diamond in the center. Yet no clothes, handsome as they were, could compare in beauty with his glorious manhood. Never had she seen so fair a mortal.

Happy was the bride whose feelings were thus changed in a moment from repulsion and horror to warmest affection and strongest veneration. The next morning when, to the amazement of his foster-father and mother, Mr. and Mrs. Pak, the prince presented himself and his bride at breakfast, he told the story of his life. As son of the King of the Stars he had committed some offense, in punishment for which his father condemned him to live upon the earth in the form of a frog. Furthermore he had laid upon his son the duty of performing three tasks. These must be done before he should be allowed to come back and live in Star Land. These were, to drink up all the water in the lake, to eat all the fish, and to win a human bride, the handsomest woman in the world.

All the precious things which he had presented to Pak and his wife to make their old days comfortable, and the gifts sent to the bride's house before her wedding-day, had come by power from the skies. Now, leaving his foster-parents on earth to enjoy their gifts, he must return home to his father, taking his bride with him. Scarcely had he spoken these words than a chariot and horses, silver bright, appeared at the door of the house. Bowing low to his foster-parents, and stepping in with his bride, the pair disappeared beyond the clouds.

From this time forth a new double star was seen in the sky.

SHOES FOR HATS

Many centuries ago when Korea was named Chosen, or the Land of Morning Splendor, the island-kingdom out in the eastern sea, where the sun rises, was called The Land of the Dragon-Fly; which some foolish people call "the Devil's Darning Needle," because its body is so slender, its wings so wide and its eyes so big. The Koreans called these islanders "dwarfs," because they were not tall of stature, though they were very warlike and brave. The isle men had no books or letters, and were very rude in their manners.

Therefore, many kind teachers, filled with the spirit of Great Buddha, crossed the sea, from Everlasting Great Korea, to teach these islanders politeness, and how to read and write, and to build pagodas, and temples and schools.

This is the reason why these islanders, who had no story books or writing before the coming of the Korean teachers, have no ancient history of what happened long, long ago when Korea was a great country. So the grandmothers in the islands used to tell their children the good old fairy tales, which many elderly people know by heart, and can relate without reading, thinking that the kings and queens they talked about were real people, when they were only dreams.

The islanders call their country The Land Where the Day Begins, and there are many fairies in these islands, some good, some bad.

So today, these island people make pictures in books and plays on the stage, and "movies" about these Koreans. They get up tableaux and pageants to tell how first the fairies and the King's servants from these far off islands, long ago came to Korea. They wanted to learn politeness, how to make and wear the proper kind of clothes, and how to draw and paint, how to make pictures, how to build houses, how to dance and sing, and make music and play on instruments, how to teach and have schools. For the good fairies always like to do pretty things.

Yet instead of being grateful for what they had received from Korea, there was one of these island people, a famous woman, who was envious because she lived in a poor land while the Koreans had a rich and beautiful country. Instead of swamps and grassy plains, with plenty of wild beasts and birds, and only a few people, poor and miserable, Korea was rich in rice fields and orchards full of fruit. Flowers grew in plenty. Birds, deer, and rabbits were numerous in the mountains and the scenery was beautiful.

In the warm waters millions of fat fish swam and were easily caught. So the people had plenty of food to eat. Down along the bottom of the sea were most lovely water plants of rich colors, yellow, purple, green and white, with sea weeds, corals and sponges. In some of the sea caves lurked the giant crabs, cuttle-fish and every sort of marine monster.

Still further down, below, deeper than any line could fathom, dwelt the Dragon King of the World Under the Sea and his Queen, with genii and dragons, and all her attendant maidens. These made sweet music, and here amid the mermaids the fairies had a happy time.

These islanders had priests who went down by the seaside when the tide was low. There they called on the spirits of the deep to grant them a safe voyage, good luck, victory over the Koreans, and safe return. There they stood and watched the rippling waves as the breezes blew over the sea.

The first living thing that poked its nose above the waters was the guardian of the seashore and the tides, called the Salt Water Giant. He came up with his head all covered with clam and oyster shells, sea weed, shrimps and whatever grows in the sand or bottom of the ocean. He had to push aside hundreds of white jelly fish that bumped against him, as the clumsy old chap made his way up to the surface and then waded to the shore.

Now this giant fairy was a grumpy sort of a fellow, and seeing the Queen and her soldiers he growled out: "What do you want?"

Very politely the Queen's messenger made a soft answer to the big fellow and begged him to announce to his master, the Dragon King of the World Under the Sea, that the Queen wished him to help her.

Would he please order all the great fish and every sea monster to go ahead and pull her ship forward?

Would he also present her with the two sparkling tide-jewels, which govern the ebb and the flood tides? If he would do so, then, in the one case her enemies might be overwhelmed. In the other case, the ships of the Koreans would be left high and dry on the shore. Then she could march through the country and get all the gold and gems, and furs and jewels, and clothes and nice things to eat, and bring them back to her own country.

With the tide jewels in her hand she could certainly conquer.

"And if you please, one thing more," added the messenger.

"What else do you want?" growled the Salt Water Giant.

"Have your master, the Dragon King, give our queen power to capture many hundreds of the Korean artists, craftsmen, teachers, and men of books and letters. We shall make these men prisoners and bring them to our country and be civilized."

"And what will you do in return to me and my master for all this?" roared the Salt Water Giant. His voice was like a booming cannon for he was as mad as fire.

"As soon as we get back safely to these shores, our Queen will build a temple in honor of the Dragon King. We shall burn incense to him, and our people will pay him our devotions."

"Well then, what else?" roared the Salt Water Giant.

"There will be a shrine also dedicated to you, my lord, and we'll get the best Korean artists to decorate it it in wave patterns, with drops of foam."

The Salt Water Giant bowed and disappeared with a tremendous splash. Down, down, down, he went to report to his master, the Dragon King of the World Under the Sea.

It was necessary for the dignity of His Majesty, that the Queen and her soldiers should wait until flood tide; for the Dragon King never appeared except at high water. So the Queen's servant launched her ship and waited out on the waves for the answer they hoped to get.

No sooner did the tide mark on the sea beach show that the

waves had reached the highest point of flood tide, than the sea opened. The white foam curled round the Queen's ship while all on board held their breath, to see what was coming. They knew they would soon behold a sight to make them shiver, for the great deep was mightily stirred.

First rose into view a terrible dragon's head, on the helmet of the King. It had eyes that seemed to flash fire. Then His Majesty appeared. In a great sea shell, as big as a bushel and held in both hands, he had the two tide jewels.

These he presented to the Queen and then quickly disappeared beneath the waves. The last thing they saw was the dragon's head, which, besides the two eyes like lightning, had teeth that could bite a boat in half, even when full of men. This monster could swallow down the whole crew in his mouth, that was as wide as a man-eating shark's. His enormously long black moustaches were as stout as ships' cables.

Immediately after receiving the tide jewels, the Queen of the barbarians landed on the southern coast of Korea. After a few weeks, having fought many battles with the Koreans, she made them bring to her their gold, jewels, furs, fans, rice and pretty things.

She and her people cared nothing about slaves, or common prisoners, but whenever and wherever they could find a painter, an artist, a costumer, a maker of pottery, or a man of books, or a priest, they seized and took him along. They carried over with them, to the island, a great treasure of gems, gold, ornaments and pretty clothes. They also took away many seeds of flowers and fruit trees, such as lemons, oranges, apples and pears.

In the islands to which they came, these smart men of skill and knowledge from Korea taught the islanders, who had lived like gypsies or Indians, how to build houses, palaces, and temples, to make fine clothes, to paint pictures, and to be like the Koreans and Chinese who knew all about these things. So the islands became rich in fruit, rice, grain, pagodas and temples. After this the island people wore lovely clothes, and had fine manners.

Now the islanders were great borrowers. They invented very few things themselves, but depended on their neighbors for much of what they had. So they filled both their heads and pockets from what they had brought from Korea. But they often made funny mistakes. When they wanted to learn about fine manners and fine clothes, they asked what, on solemn occasions, and in time of ceremony, they should put on their heads.

The Koreans were greatly offended at these savages from over the sea for invading their country and taking away their artists and craftsmen. So they now resolved to play a trick on the islanders.

So when men from the isles in the ocean sent a company of men to Korea and asked for caps to put on their heads, and be shown how do to things properly, the Koreans in contempt gave them their old shoes, which had strings on them to tie over their feet.

But the islanders, who loved to go about with little clothing on their backs, and usually went barefoot, did not know what these shoes were. They thought these were some kind of head-gear, hats or bonnets.

So they put them on their heads like skull caps and tied them with the white strings down under their chins. These were like tapes and held the caps on around their necks.

So to this day the islanders, when making offerings to the fairies, wear this head-gear and think their shoe-caps are very fine.

THE VOICE OF THE BELL

When Tai Jo, the great general and first King of Korea, founded a new dynasty, he moved the capital near the great river Han and resolved to build a mighty city called Han Yang, or the Castle on the Han. It was to have a high wall around it and lofty gates on each side. However, the people commonly called the city Seoul, or Capital. All the roads in the kingdom lead to it.

Happy was he when the workmen, in digging for the foundations of the East Gate, came upon a bell. It was a lucky omen and they carried it at once to the king. He had it suspended over the entrance to his palace and there it still hangs.

But such a bell could only tinkle, while King Tai Jo wanted one that would boom loud and long. He was especially anxious about this, for in Silla, once a rival state, there had hung for centuries one of the biggest bells in the world and Tai Jo wanted one that excelled even that famed striker of the hours. He would have even a larger bell to hang in the central square in the heart of Seoul, that could be heard by every man, woman and child in the city. After that, it must be able to flood miles of hill and valley with its melody. By this sound the people would know when to get up, cook their breakfast, sit down to supper, or go to bed. On special occasions his subjects would know when a king's procession was passing, or a royal prince or princess was being married. It would sound out a dirge when, His Majesty being dead, all the land must mourn and the people wear white clothes for three years and Korea becomes the land of mourners. The guardian spirit of the city would have its home in the bell.

Word was sent out by messengers who rode on big horses, little ponies, donkeys and bulls to all the provinces, publishing the king's command to all governors, magistrates and village-heads to collect the copper and tin to make the bronze metal. The bell was to stand ten feet above the ground and be eight feet across; that is, as high and wide as a Korean bedroom. On the top, forming the framework, by which the bell was to be hung, were to be two terrible looking dragons. Weighing so many tons that it would balance five hundred fat men on a seesaw, only

heavy beams made of whole tree-trunks could hold it in the belfry, which must be strong enough to stand the shaking when the monster was rung. It had no clapper inside, but without, swung by heavy ropes from pulleys above, was a long log. This, men pulled back and then let fly, striking the boss on the bell's surface. This awoke the music of the bell, making it toll, boom, rumble, growl, hum, croak, or roll sweet melody, according as the old bellman desired.

So the procession of bullock carts on the roads to Seoul creaked with the ingots of copper. Many a donkey had swallowed gallons of bean soup at the inn stables before he dropped his load of metal in the city, while hundreds of bulls bellowed under their weight of the brushwood and timber piled on their backs to feed the furnaces, which were to melt the alloy for the casting of the mighty bell.

Deep was the pit dug to hold the core and mould, and hundreds of fire-clay pots and ladles were made ready for use when the red-hot stream should be ready to flow. All the boys in Seoul were waiting to watch the fire kindle, the smoke rise, the bellows roar, the metal run, and the foreman give the signal to tap.

When the fire-imp in the volcano heard of what was going on, he was awfully jealous, not thinking ever that common men could handle so much metal, direct properly such roaring flames, and cast so big a bell. He snorted at the idea that King Tai Jo's men could beat the bells that hung in China's mighty temples or in Silla's pagodas.

But when there was not yet enough and the copper collectors were still at their work, one of them came to a certain village and called at a house where lived an old woman carrying a baby boy strapped to her back. She had no coin, cash, metal, or fuel to give, but was quite ready to offer either herself or the baby. In a tone that showed her willingness, she said:

"May I give you this boy?"

The collector paid no attention to her, but passed on, taking nothing from the old woman. When in Seoul, however, he told the story. Thus it came to pass that many heard of the matter and remembered it later.

So when all was ready, the fire-clay crucibles were set on the white-hot coals. The blast roared until the bronze metal turned to liquid. Then, at the word of the master, the hissing, molten stream ran out and filled the mould. Patiently waiting till the metal cooled, alas! they found the bell cracked.

The casting was raised by means of heavy tackle, erected at great expense on the spot, and the bell was broken up into bits by stalwart blacksmiths, wielding heavy hammers. Then a second casting was made, but again, when cool, it was found to be cracked.

Three separate times this happened, until the price of a palace had been paid for work, fuel, and wages, and yet there was no bell. King Tai Jo was in despair. Yet, instead of crying, or pulling his topknot, or berating the artisans, who had done the best they could, he offered a large reward to any one who could point out where the trouble lay, or show what was lacking, and thus secure a perfect casting. Thereupon out stepped a workman from the company, who told the story of the old woman and said that the bell would crack after every cooling unless her proposal was accepted. Anyway, he said, the hag was a sorceress, and if the child were not a real human being no harm could be done.

So the baby boy was sent for and, when the liquid metal had half filled the pit, was thrown into the mass. There was some feeling about "feeding a child to the fire demon," but when they hoisted the cooled bell up from the mould, lo, the casting was a perfect success and every one apparently forgot about the human life that had entered the bell. Soon with file and chisel, the great work was finished. The hanging ceremonies were very impressive when the bell was put in place on the city's central square, where the broad streets from the South Gate and those looking to sunrise and sunset met together. Suspended by heavy iron links from the staple on a stout timber frame, the bell's mouth was exactly a foot above ground. Then, around and over it, was built the belfry. The names of the chief artisans who cast the bell and of the royal officers who superintended the hanging ceremonies were engraved on the metal. It was decided, however, not to strike the bell until it was fully housed and the sounder or suspended log of wood, as thick as the mast of a ship, was made ready to send forth the initial boom.

Meanwhile tens of thousands of people waited to hear the first music of the bell. Every one believed it to be good luck and that they would live the longer for it. The boys and girls could hardly go to bed for listening, and some were afraid they might be asleep when it boomed. The little folks, whose eyes were usually fast shut at sunset, begged hard to stay up that night until they could hear the bell, but some fell asleep, because they could not help it, and their eyes closed before they knew it.

"What shall the name of the bell be, your Majesty?" asked a wise counselor.

"Call it In Jung," said King Tai Jo. "That means 'Man Decides,' for every night, at nine o'clock, let every man or boy decide to go to bed. Except magistrates, let not one male person be found in the street on pain of being paddled. From that hour until midnight the women shall have the streets to themselves to walk in." The royal law was proclaimed by trumpeters and it was ordained also that every morning and evening, at sunrise and sunset, the band of music should play at the opening and shutting of the city gates.

So In Jung, or "Masculine Decision," is the bell's name to this day.

But as yet the bell was silent. It had not spoken. When it did sound, the Seoul people discovered that it was the most wonderful bell ever cast. It had a memory and a voice. It could wail, as well as sing. In fact, some to this day declare it can cry; for, whether in childhood, youth, middle or old age, in joy or gladness, the bell expresses their own feelings by its change of note, lively or gay, in warning or congratulation.

At nine o'clock in the first night of the seventh moon- the month of the Star Maiden of the Loom and the Ox-boy with his train of attendants, who stand on opposite sides of the River of Heaven and cross over on the bridge of birds, the great bell of Seoul was to be sounded. All the men were in their rooms ready to undress and go to bed at once, while all the women, fully clothed in their best, were on the door-steps ready, each with her lantern in hand, for their promenade outdoors.

Four strong men seized the rope, pulled back the striking log a whole yard's distance and then let fly. Back bounded the timber and out gushed a flood of melody that rolled across the city in every direction, and over the hills, filling leagues of space with sweet sound. The children clapped their hands and danced with joy. They knew they would live long, for they had heard the sweet bell's first music. The old people smiled with joy.

But what was the surprise of the adult folks to hear that the bell could talk. Yes, its sounds actually made a sentence.

"Mu-u-u-ma-ma-ma-la-la-la-la-la-la- - " until it ended like a baby's cry. Yes! There was no mistake about it. This is what it said:

"My mother's fault. My mother's fault."

And to this day the mothers in Seoul, as they clasp their darlings to their bosoms, resolve that it shall be no fault of theirs if these lack love or care. They delight in their little ones more, and lavish on them a tenderer affection because they hear the great bell talk, warning parents to guard what Heaven has committed to their care.

THE KING OF THE SPARROWS

The Korean children are awakened every morning by the twittering of the sparrows. These little birds build their nests among the vines on the roof and along the eaves. The people plant melon, gourd, and mock orange seeds along the sunny sides of their houses in spring time. All through the summer, and until late in autumn, the walls and roofs are covered with the thick green leaves. Here, in these sheltered places, the sparrow mother lays her eggs and the father sparrow finds worms and feeds her, until the hungry birdies open their little mouths for something to eat. After this, both parents are kept busy in raising their brood and teaching them to fly.

The greatest dangers to the birdlings come from cruel snakes that live on the roof and eat up the young sparrows. Sometimes, to help them against their enemy, the parent sparrows call in the aid of larger birds that are not afraid of the reptiles. These peck at the snake until they drive him away. There is always a lively chattering over the victory.

One day, a young sparrow that had hardly learned to fly was almost seized, and might have been devoured by the roof-snake, but was saved by a big, brave bird that flew at the reptile. Although escaped from the snake's jaws, the sparrow in falling caught its legs in the curtain made of split bamboo, which hung before the verandah of the house, and its limb was put out of joint. There it lay helpless between the splints.

The owner of the house was a kind man, who loved the birds. Taking pity on the poor sparrow, he carefully lifted it up, smoothed its feathers, and quieted the little creature, while its heart kept beating so fast. Then setting its leg in place, he put some moist clay around the broken part, until it should be all right again. Meanwhile, he kept it warm, feeding the birdie until it was strong again. One day he took it in his hand and out-of-doors letting it fly away. Soon it came back and perched on the edge of the roof, twittering thanks to its kind friend. Then it spread its wings to fly to the King of the Sparrows, who lived in the city of Sparrow Capital, where it at once informed

His Majesty about the good man who healed and befriended birds when they were in trouble and who had saved the young sparrow's life.

The King of Sparrow Land and all his wise counselors heard the story with great interest. Then they held a meeting and voted to reward richly so good a friend of all sparrows. So they went into the storehouse where were kept beautiful treasures which human beings love. From the collection they chose what they thought would please most their good friend, such as gold, jade, brocade, cups and saucers, rice, horses to ride on, oxen to bear heavy loads and pretty maids to wait on him, besides silk and cotton clothes of all sorts, with delicious things to eat and drink. By some magic process, they packed these into a seed and then gave it to the sparrow in its bill to carry to the good man. They charged the bird on no account to lose it and be sure to give it to no one but the right person.

So the sparrow flew out of Sparrow Land and down to the house of its kind friend. Carefully laying down the seed, it kept near the paper window-frame and made a great twittering, until the man came out to see what was the matter. Recognizing his old acquaintance, he put out his open hand and the sparrow laid the seed in his palm, meanwhile chattering in a lively way and looking in his face as if to tell him how precious the treasure was.

But the good fellow only took it in to his wife and told her how he got it, laughed over the matter and was going to throw it away, thinking it only sparrow fun.

The wife, who was a wise woman, begged her husband to keep it and on a warm day in spring she planted it. It grew to be a luxuriant vine that clothed all one side of the house with its leaves. When one unusually fine large handsome gourd was nearly ripe, the man thought of plucking it for food; but, taking his wife's advice, he waited until full autumn had come. By this time the gourd, having absorbed the sunshine all summer, was fully ripe.

Then they took a saw to open it properly, and lo! a store of riches came out of that gourd, such as neither the man nor his wife had ever dreamed of.

First issued something which spread itself out before them. It was a table of costly jade, such as an Emperor ever eats from. Next rolled forth a silver bottle of delicious wine and then the daintiest cups, that set themselves on the jade table. Soon a gold tea-caddy appeared filled with the fragrant leaf. Then rolls of silk, fine muslin, satin brocade, and a store of rich clothes, hats, shoes, girdles, and socks enough to last a lifetime appeared before their eyes. After these were rice and cooked food of all sorts ready for a feast. Looking out into the yard, they saw strong horses and fat oxen waiting to do their master's bidding. Last of all, some lovely young girls, as fair as the moon, stepped out of the gourd and proceeded to serve the good things of the feast, as if they had been used to waiting on ladies and gentlemen all their lives. Following the feast, they danced, made music and gave no end of entertainment and service to the man and his wife, who were now as happy as king and queen.

In their once humble home, now made over new, with all the store of good things and plenty of loyal servants and strong animals to serve them, the old couple lived without care and traveled where they pleased.

But when a wicked man, that hated all sparrows and had often driven them away from his house, because he thought them too troublesome, heard of his neighbor's good fortune, he was envious, and wanted to get riches in the same way. So he watched his opportunity and, when a sparrow came near, he threw a stick at the bird and broke its leg. Then he bound up the limb with clay and a bit of rag. He kept the poor sparrow until its leg was well, but dreadfully crooked, and then let it fly away.

In the capital of Sparrow Land, the poor bird told about the bad man's doings. The Sparrow King at once handed out a seed to be given to the enemy of the sparrows. When the naughty man saw the little bird with the crooked legs, he ran out, got the seed and planted it at once. He could hardly wait for the gourd to ripen. Wonderful to relate, however, the vine was most luxurious, covering the whole side of the house and all the thatched roofs of the three dwellings in one, which made up his home. Finally in the autumn he plucked the fruit. Then, sitting down before the pile, with knife and saw, he began to open them.

But instead of good things, and lovely people, and the treasures that make men rich and happy, such as his kind neighbor had received, there came out, one after another, the twelve curses of Korea.

First leaped forth a party of rope dancers, who put out their hands and demanded money. They threatened to live with him and eat at his table unless they got their pay.

There was no help for it. So the cruel man had to give each dancer a long string of cash before he could get rid of the party.

No sooner had he opened the second gourd than out stepped a line of Buddhist priests, who at once began begging for the temples. He was only too glad to buy off these shaven pates.

The saw had no sooner let the light into another gourd, than forth came a band of hired mourners carrying a corpse. They began weeping, wailing and crying out loud enough to waken the dead. It required another rope of cash to get rid of these pests. By this time the cruel man was beginning to feel very poor.

Almost afraid to touch the other gourds, but still greedily hoping for riches, he sawed them open; but one after the other yielded only what took his money and threatened to make him a beggar. From the fourth gourd issued a bevy of dancing girls, who refused to leave the house until he had paid them five thousand cash. From another gourd a pair of acrobats leaped out and began a performance. But knowing that they would charge the more for their tricks, if they were allowed to finish their program, the man bought them off as he had done the others.

Getting poorer and poorer, with no sign of wealth coming from the gourds, he yet felt he must open more, but the result was the same. The strangest people, men and women, such as loafers from the government offices, fortune-tellers, jugglers, and blind folks appeared. These last had sticks in their hands to find the way, and bells at their belts to collect alms. Finally, of all living things, a giant stood forth, that threatened to eat up both the man and his wife.

By this time there was not a coin or a cash left, and, besides being as poor as a rat, the man was hungry. When the twelfth gourd was opened it seemed to have in it all the smells of Korea. Holding their noses, the man and his wife ran out of their house. Happily for them that they did so, for just then a gale of wind blew down the house, and the thatch and timbers burst into flames from the fire that had heated the flues.

Thus stripped of all their possessions, because of the man's cruelty to the birds, the wicked fellow and his wife would have starved, except for the kindness of the good man who treated the sparrows kindly. For the rest of their days the old couple lived on their neighbor's charity.

THE WOODMAN AND THE MOUNTAIN FAIRIES

Over a half thousand years ago there lived in a northern village, near Ping Yang, a wood-cutter named Keel Wee.

He owned a sturdy bull that carried on its back the fuel which he daily cut on the mountains and sold on the main street of his village, at the fair, which was held every fifth day. The docile brute could carry a load of faggots and brushwood piled many feet high over his head and tied down with ropes, so that at a distance nothing but his legs were visible. This beast, although so huge, was the gentlest creature imaginable. The children were all very fond of the big fellow and were accustomed to play with him as if he were one of them, or at least like a pet dog. The reason of this was that when but a week old the bull-calf had been taken from his cow-mother and brought up in the family with the girls and boys. Only the puppy dog, that also occupied the house with the young folks, was a great favorite.

On a fine summer morning, Keel Wee, leaving his beast behind, went up on the mountain and cut enough wood to load up and bring down on another day.

His wife, as she shouted good-bye, told him to be sure and be home in time for supper, for their eldest son had gone a-fishing and a good string of perch was expected.

Shouldering his axe, he started up the mountain path. He had to go pretty far, for near towns or cities in Korea all the timber had long since been cut away. Every year the woodmen have to search farther afield to find fuel.

Arriving in the woods where there was a clearing, Keel Wee prepared to wield his trusty axe. He was about to take off his big hat and outer coat and lay about him, when he spied, at some distance off, two fairy-like beings. They had long hair, looked very wise and were dressed in costume of the Chow dynasty of two thousand years ago. They sat on stones and played the game of go-ban.

Coming near, the woodman took a respectful attitude, and, looking on, soon became interested in the moves of the players.

So far from being at all disconcerted at the presence of a stranger, the two fairies seemed by eye-winks to invite him to look on. Feeling quite proud to be thus honored, Keel Wee, leaning his chin upon the handle of his axe, became absorbed in the game and by and by grew quite excited. Forgetting himself and his manners, he stretched forth his right hand to move one of the pieces. At once the fairy nearest to him gave him a crack on the fingers for his impudence, and jerked Keel Wee's arm away. Then without saying a word, he took out from his wallet something that looked like a persimmon seed and put in the woodman's mouth. After this all three were perfectly quiet.

Hour after hour the game proceeded and the players grew more intensely interested. As for Keel Wee, his eyes never winked, so hard did he look at the yellow board covered with the black and white pieces. Several times, when he thought he saw how the fairy on his right could beat in the game, or the one on his left make a better move, he felt like telling one or the other so. When, however, he tried to move his tongue, he found he could not speak, or utter a cry. Somehow he felt as if he were in a dream.

Yet all the time he became more and more wrapped up in the game, so that he determined to see the end of it and know which player had beaten. He forgot that with mountain spirits there is no night or morning, or passing of the hours, nor do they care anything about clocks or bells, because in fairy-land there is no time.

All the while Keel Wee was leaning with his chin on the stout axe-handle, holding it with both hands under his neck. He took no note of the sun or stars, daylight or darkness and he felt no hunger.

Suddenly the timber of his axe seemed to turn to dust and his chin fell. The next thing he knew he had lost his support. Down went his head, and forward fell his body as he tumbled over, upsetting the checker-board, breaking up the game and scattering the round pieces hither and yon over the ground.

Awaking as out of a sleep, and thoroughly ashamed of himself for his impoliteness, he tried to pick himself up and humbly apologize for the accident which he had caused by his own rudeness. He expected and was ready for a good scolding. But when he looked up, the fairies were gone. Nothing whatever was seen of them or of the playboard and checkers, nor any signs of their having been there, except that when he put his hand on the flat stones, which they had used as seats, he found them warm to his touch.

But where was his axe-handle and what had happened? When he had left home, he had come straight from the barber shop, with his face smooth and clean shaven. Now he put his hand to his breast and found that he had grown a long white beard. As for the iron axe-head, it was there, but rusty and half buried in the ground. He had worn one of the big farmer's hats, which, when turned upside down, might hold a bushel or two of turnips, and when fastened to his head spread over his shoulders like a roof. Where could it be? He looked about him to find it, but saw only the bits of the slats inside the frame and a few scraps of what remained, for the rest had long ago rotted away. Meanwhile he had discovered that his joints were stiff, and he felt like an old man. His clothes were a mass of rags, his hemp sandals were no more, and, on both fingers and toes, had grown long nails like bird's claws. His hair had burst its topknot string and hung down his back like a woman's, only it was grayish-white.

Wondering what it all meant, Keel Wee hobbled down the mountain and found the road that ran into the main street of his village. Rocks and hills, rivers and rills were there, but what a change! Instead of the two grinning idol posts, of male and female faces, carved out of trunks and trees, with sawed-out teeth painted white, and artificial ear flaps of wood nailed on, such as had stood before every Korean hamlet since the days of Kija, there was a line of high thick poles, with iron wire stretching from one to the other and for miles in the distance. These, he found out afterward, were called "lightning-thread-trees" (telegraph poles). In place of the rambling and sprawling three-sided thatched houses and yards, divided off with mats hung from sticks, there was a well-built but odd-looking office of painted wood, with openings through which he saw Korean young men sitting. They were dressed in strange clothes and were fingering outlandish-looking clicking instruments.

His curiosity prompted him to go up and look more closely,

when something bumped against his nose and nearly knocked him over. When he tried again to get closer, his face was flattened, his nose nearly broken, and his lips knocked against his teeth so that they swelled. Feeling with his hands to solve the mystery, he touched something hard, which he could yet see through. Just then he heard a young man inside shout to him in Korean:

"Here, you mountain daddy, let that glass alone."

"Glass? Glass?" thought Keel Wee. "What is that?" Yet he could not speak.

He had hardly drawn a long breath when, looking down along two lines of shining iron in the street, he saw a house on wheels coming right at him. There was no horse, no donkey, no bull, no man pulling or pushing it, but overhead was a long pole, at the end of which, where it touched a string, as he thought, though it was an iron wire, was something that looked like a squirrel. It was going round and round as if turning somersaults and seemed to be pushing the moving house along. Inside, near the same stuff which he had already heard was glass, sat a dozen or so Koreans. The whole thing, wheels and all, nearly ran over him as it thundered by, and his mouth opened in wonder, while a man on the end shouted rudely:

"Hello, old goblin, where did you get your pumpkin mouth? Look out or you'll swallow the moon. Get out of the way of the trolley."

Thus did the man they called conductor, or guard, make fun of the poor old fellow, for indeed he did look like one of the mummers, who on New Year's Eve amuse or scare the children by putting on their shoulders the huge round devil heads and false faces that represent the aborigines of Korea and the goblins that once lived in the mountains. These masks are usually shaped like a melon and are cut with eyes, nose and mouth, like those which American boys have fun with on All Hallow Eve.

This was just the trouble. The woodman in tatters, with no topknot, long hair down his back and a white beard floating over his breast, leaning on a long white stick as he hobbled down the street, looked just like one of the ancient aborigines that had long ago been driven into the mountains. Nurses and old women frightened naughty children by simply mentioning their names. When one of these mountain men, odd creatures that were half savage in dress and ways, came into the town, all the children laughed and the big dogs barked, while the little ones ran away, for the sight was so unusual. Even the bulls bellowed, the donkeys balked, and the pigs squeaked, as Keel Wee came near. No wonder he was taken for a mountain granddaddy, or a bumpkin dressed up like one, for few of the city or village folks had really ever seen one of the mountain aborigines, any more than they had seen tigers, that are plentiful farther away, but which only the hunters ever caught sight of.

More and more bewildered, Keel Wee wended his way further into the town. He saw that the men no longer wore topknots, or chignons, nor did the lads have on the long braid down their back, which showed that they were youths, but not married yet. Just then some rough boys, supposing that maybe some rustic gawk had mistaken the time of year, jeered at him and cried:

"Hello, hermit, do you think it's New Year's Eve?"

Keel Wee thought he had better ask some questions. So catching sight of a dignified looking gentleman, in black broad-brimmed hat and flowing white clothes, who was coming down the street and toward him, Keel Wee bowed his head low, almost to the ground. As he did so, the stone put in his mouth by the fairies dropped out, and his tongue was loosed. He inquired as follows:

"Exalted sir, can you tell me where may be the wretched hut of my miserable wife and children? She was the daughter of Gee Kim, and your contemptible slave is Keel Wee."

The gentleman, whose dress showed that he was a scholar and person of rank, looked long and hard at the questioner, to satisfy himself that he was not being mocked, or imposed upon by a jester, rope-dancer, sorcerer, or some such disreputable person, and then cried:

"Heavens! man, are you a beggar-spirit of the mountains?

Your speech sounds like the dialect spoken in these parts five hundred years ago. In that time such a family lived here, but the head of it, a wood-cutter and fuel-seller, is reported to have gone up into the mountains and was eaten up by a tiger. Yonder in the graveyard are buried ten or more generations of his descendants."

"Tell me, kind sir, what has happened here since King Wang died. It was under his reign that I was born and lived in this village."

Still eyeing the questioner, as if expecting to see him jump out of his rags and declare himself a mummer and the whole affair a joke, the kindly gentleman proceeded to give in outline the history of Korea during the previous five hundred years. There had been many kings. The Tartars first, and then the Japanese had invaded the land. A great war between the Mikado's men and the Chinese had taken place. It was just over and now people rode in cars, talked hundreds of miles over wires, and traveled over iron rails as fast as a dragon could fly, drawn by a steel horse that drank water and fed on wood and black stones that burned. In a word, Korea was in an "era of civilization."

This was too much for Keel Wee. He now realized that he had lived ten times longer than the average man. So, hobbling over to the graveyard, he stumbled among the mounds until he found that one of his clan where the bones of his wife and children lay. Next morning, all that was seen of Keel Wee was a mass of dust, rags, some bones, and much long white hair. Yet, when they buried him, there sprang up around and on his grave strange flowers that no one had ever seen in city or village, but which bloomed only on the high mountains.

THE END

ABOUT AUTOR

William Elliot Griffis was an American author, educator, and minister, known for his contributions to the study of Japanese and Korean culture. He was born on September 17, 1843, in Philadelphia, Pennsylvania.

Griffis developed a strong interest in Asia and its cultures from a young age. He studied at Rutgers University and later at Union Theological Seminary, where he became ordained as a minister. In 1870, he embarked on a journey to Japan as a missionary.

During his time in Japan, Griffis immersed himself in the local culture and language. He taught at various schools and universities, including the Imperial Japanese Naval Academy. He also became an advocate for modern education and Western influences in Japan, playing a significant role in the country's early modernization efforts.

Griffis's passion for Japanese culture led him to write numerous books and articles on the subject. His works covered a wide range of topics, including history, folklore, and travel. One of his notable works is «The Mikado's Empire,» a comprehensive study of Japan's history and culture.

Later in his career, Griffis also turned his attention to Korean culture. He published «Korean Fairy Tales» in 1922, a collection of traditional Korean folktales that introduced Western readers to the rich storytelling heritage of Korea.

Throughout his life, William Elliot Griffis made significant contributions to the understanding and appreciation of Japanese and Korean culture in the Western world. He passed away on February 5, 1928, leaving behind a legacy of scholarship and cultural exchange.

Printed in Great Britain
by Amazon